COYOTE CANYON

A Brock Clemons Western

Book Three

Scott Harris

Foreword From Robert Hanlon

When writing Westerns, I often wonder what it would be like to truly capture the magic of the Old West. What would it feel like to bottle up a moment in that frenzied time? I think Harris comes close to selling his own brand of the West—bottled up for people to enjoy, over and over again. If it were up to me, I'd have him writing his stories of the Old West every single day with a new book for release each week. He's got it!

~ Robert Hanlon – Bestselling western author of "<u>Clint Cain</u>*" and "*<u>The Guns of Clint Cain</u>*"*

Foreword From M. Allen

This new release from Scott Harris has been sitting on my desk for a couple of weeks now. What can one say about a writer with such talent? Harris has taken the Western to the next level with "Coyote Creek." A masculine writing style, filled with action, drama and all the vigor of the Old West. This is definitely one of the Westerns I would pick up for 2018!

~ M. Allen – Bestselling author of "Will's Revenge" and many other Western adventures.

A Readers Note From David Watts

The first thing you notice is a sense of immediacy. As readers we are in the story instantly and curious about it. It is as if we are are participants in the action, contributors to the decision making, a relationship that gives us the right to agree or disagree with what is going on and thereby learn something about ourselves in the process. It is the sign of a good writer that he can make us do that.

The next thing I noticed was that there is a little trace of mystery here and there. The mind loves a mystery, a puzzle to solve, an answer to wait for over the pages and story fragments that greet us. It keeps us hooked in while the writer deepens the reach of the narrative.

His writing takes us into the mind of the character quite a bit. To hear the character talking, telling us not only his parts of the story but a lot about how he thinks the way he does, gives us the psychological backdrop that allows us to enter his actions with a much wider understanding of reasons and consequences. What remains are the little surprises that make us change our perception and add yet another chamber to the cave of the interior mind.

Add to that an authentic understanding of the terrain, the animals and their behaviors, the unpredictability of weather and human nature and you've got a story that you might well remember long after it is done.

Enjoy the journey.

*~ David Watts – Author of the #1 bestseller "**<u>The Guns of Pecos County</u>**" and top ten sequel "**<u>The Long Ride</u>**."*

Dedication

I would like to dedicate this book to my two favorite authors: John Steinbeck and Mark Twain. They inspired me to read, ignited my imagination and motivated me to dream and travel, and eventually, they fueled my love for writing.

Coyote Pups

"Chavez, you talk about killing as if it's easy. It isn't. But I don't think you know that. I know you have Diego and a couple of others with you. And you hide behind them like you do those rocks, like all cowards do. When I think of you, I think of a man who, on his own ranch, when he still had a ranch, even when surrounded by all his hired guns— including you Diego—backed down to one man, me. And now, I watch as the four of you hide away in the hills like scared coyote pups, talking big, but with nothing left but talk, not even the cattle you stole."

One - Brock

The calendar says it's early spring, but the weather hasn't quite let go of winter. The sun is falling quickly—along with the temperature—and it's starting to feel like this might be the coldest night of an already cold trip. Supper, a fire and especially a hot cup of coffee sound even better than they usually do as I button up my jacket against the first few flakes of snow.

We've been on the trail for a week, which is the longest I've been gone since making Dry Springs my home. I must be getting a little soft, since before last fall I'd spent more than two years on the trail and usually felt pretty good, and now, after only a week—and not a hard week at that—I'm a little sore, and tired. Even Horse seems to be feeling the effects of living the easy life, and I realize that when we get home, I'm going to need to ride her a bit more often to keep both of us in trail shape. I miss Sophie, of course, and I'm excited to get home and see her, but it's clear that after a few months of town living, I've also grown quite used to a front porch rocking chair, a comfortable bed and all of the other trappings of indoor living. And while it feels good to be back out on the trail, I have to admit, it feels even better to know we'll be home tomorrow.

Laughing, Frank and Cisco suddenly take off at a full gallop, each determined to end their week-long, good-natured debate by proving they have the fastest horse. Huck looks quickly and eagerly at me, and when I nod yes, he and Spirit are off like a shot, equally determined to prove both Frank and Cisco wrong. Horse and I have run enough races against Indian ponies, with far more at stake than bragging rights, that we decide to stay back and continue riding along at our leisurely pace. I don't know for certain that Horse could beat all three of them, or even any of them, though I suspect she could. I do know that if I was being chased by a handful of Apaches, with guns blazing, arrows flying, and a couple of long miles to run before reaching the relative safety of the foothills and a protective rock outcropping, there's no horse in the world I would take over Horse.

I've enjoyed the trip and everyone's company, but I'm also happy to have a few minutes alone. Even Wolf has left me, coming out of the brush and racing down the trail, keeping up with Huck and Spirit step for step. The last thing I see before they're all out of sight is Frank lose his hat, which, before it can even hit the ground, is caught up by the chilling wind and soon blown out of sight. I fasten the last couple of buttons on my coat and tug my own hat down just a little tighter, hoping to block at least some of the wind. It's a big hat, the biggest in Dry Springs, with a huge crown and a very wide brim. It stands out quite a bit more than any hat I would have chosen for myself, but since it was a Christmas present from Huck, it's the hat I've been wearing for the last few months. Every time I ask Ray why he allowed Huck to get me this particular hat—which I now suspect Ray paid for—when he has so many great hats for sale in his general store, he just looks at me and smiles. I'm told by many in town, usually with a poorly hidden grin, that it makes it easy to pick me out of a crowd or to see me coming from a long way off—not great traits in a hat whether you're out on the trail, or the town sheriff.

This is Huck's first long hunting trip, and knowing how much Sophie would miss him, it wasn't easy convincing her to let him go. But Ray said he could get by at the store for a bit without Huck, especially with Maria working there now, and Shawn and Tom agreed to pick up the extra work at the livery. And while Sophie and I both value school and his book education, she came around to agreeing that education comes in many forms and time spent on the trail, hunting and visiting our friends from the Weeminuche tribe, would also be a great learning experience. And it has been. Huck has made new friends and seen what an actual Indian camp looks like, and the hunting has been good. The pack horses are carrying three deer, five antelope, a huge elk and a few turkeys—and that doesn't count what we left behind as a gift for the Weeminuche, including a well-fed and overly aggressive black bear.

This is the first time I've visited with the Weeminuche since last fall when we rode—and fought Apaches—together at Coyote Creek. And while this is not a trip I had planned on, especially with my wedding only two weeks away, I'm glad we're doing it. It was a very pleasant surprise when Severo and Chipeta rode into Dry Springs just over a week ago. They were stopping by on the way from their home with Chipeta's Ute Muache tribe to visit Severo's Ute Weeminuche family. After only a couple of days, and not surprisingly—as much alike as they are—Chipeta and Sophie became fast friends. And when Chipeta added her voice to Severo's in asking that Huck be allowed to come on the trip, the day was won. As a matter of fact, if Sophie hadn't felt obligated to stay home and teach the other kids at Willy's Elementary School, I think she would have joined us.

Huck loved spending time on the trail and especially the two days in the Weeminuche camp, where he got to go hunting with Frank, Cisco, Arapeen and Atchee. Atchee and Cisco immediately renewed the friendship they started on the Coyote Creek trip, and it was great to see that Arapeen had completely recovered from the wounds he sustained in the Coyote Creek battle with the Apaches.

I enjoyed my conversations with Chief Ignacio, who still faces difficult challenges and painful decisions regarding the future of his people. It must be extremely hard knowing that if you don't move to a reservation, as the United States Army has demanded you do, your people will in all likelihood be wiped out in the seemingly never-ending battles with the Army, the Apaches and the Navajo, but also knowing if you do move to the reservation, you'll be leaving your culture, and the only life you've ever known or wanted, irretrievably behind. The Weeminuche are running out of time to decide, and it is easy to see that the situation is weighing heavily on the chief, who, while in good spirits, appears to have aged far more since I last saw him than the calendar would seem to indicate.

I do know Sophie will be excited that the chief, along with Severo and Chipeta, will be returning to Dry Springs for our wedding, making an already special day even more meaningful and, hopefully, giving Chief Ignacio a short, well-deserved and pleasant break from his troubles.

As I ride into camp, I can hear Frank and Cisco still arguing—and still laughing—both claiming to have won the race. Cisco is declaring that Regalo cannot be beat, and Huck, not to be outdone, is reminding everyone that he nearly caught them and that, without their head start, he and Spirit would have won. The good-natured ribbing continues as I rub Horse down with some dry grass and turn her loose for the night to find some good grazing, fresh water and Spirit, who, like Horse, rarely gets picketed. Frank and Cisco have also rubbed their horses down and have them picketed just outside of camp for the night. What was just some scattered flakes a few minutes ago has turned into a pretty steady snowfall, with a chilling wind that warns of a cold night ahead. Frank is getting our dinner going but, without his hat, is constantly having to brush snow from his head. I toss him my hat and reach into my saddlebags, grabbing a warm jacket and my extra hat. I smile at how good it feels, then glance back at Huck, feeling a little guilty.

I leave the three of them to their conversation and dinner preparation, grab all four canteens, and head down to the creek. It's too cold to take a bath, but I wash the trail off my face and get us all fresh water for tomorrow's ride home. As I walk back into camp, I can hear Huck—for at least the tenth time—telling the story of what it was like to shoot that black bear. How, on one of our many walks, he and Wolf had gone on ahead of the rest of us, alone on the trail. How Wolf had suddenly jumped in front of him, stopped walking and started growling, and before he could figure out what was happening, that old black bear came roaring out of the woods and charging, unfriendly like, toward him and Wolf. And how he expertly pulled his '49 Colt Pocket out of its holster and put three shots into that bear without even thinking, dropping him less than twenty feet from where he and Wolf were standing. The thing Huck was most proud of was how, later, back at camp, Chief Ignacio gave him his Indian name, Miwak, which means Growl of a Bear.

As Huck wraps up his bear story—which is now just about perfected for telling Tom and the other kids tomorrow, no doubt as soon as we get home to Dry Springs—I'm focused on how great this trip has been and the smell of Frank's antelope steaks and hot coffee. But the luxury of worrying about a little snow and dreaming about a hot meal and a hot cup of coffee is suddenly shattered by multiple rifle shots ringing out and Frank falling backwards, away from the fire, dead.

I immediately pull my 1858 from its holster and hit the dirt, pulling Huck down with me and rolling behind a small rock. It's too small to protect both of us, but it's the closest cover available. Turning, I can see that Cisco has made it to relative safety behind a large pine, with pistol drawn, and eyes watching for our attackers. Telling Huck not to move, I crawl over to my gear and pull my Winchester from the scabbard. I keep crawling, out of the light of the fire and toward whatever protection a small group of rocks just outside of the shadows can offer.

I look over at Huck, only a few feet away. He looks scared but has his gun drawn and is looking in the direction the shots came from. I whistle to get his attention.

"Huck, stay down and don't make a sound." He nods his agreement, and I turn toward Cisco.

Two - Brock

I can see Cisco's rifle, stacked up against his saddlebags, too close to the fire—and the light—for him to be able to risk trying to grab it. But Huck's gear is neatly laid out next to mine, away from the fire, under a huge pine tree, safe from the snow and, more importantly, safe from the light. I snap off a couple of shots to remind whoever is out there that we're still here, then quickly crawl to where Huck has set up for the night and pull his prize Christmas present, a Winchester 1866 that matches mine exactly, out of the scabbard. I roll back to the small rock where Huck is, which gets me close enough to Cisco to toss him the rifle and a box of ammo. He immediately gets off a couple of shots, and I'm grateful for the practice that he, Huck and I have been doing together every week.

A couple of shots ricochet off the small rock Huck and I are hiding behind, so either they're lucky, or they know where we are. Tired of crawling, I grab Huck and, staying low, we race the few feet back to the larger rocks. We quickly hit the dirt, relatively safe, at least for the moment. Horse and Spirit are close by, alert, but not panicked. I can hear the other two horses across camp, fortunately picketed out of the line of fire.

Huck turns to me, shivering just a little—probably as much from fear as the snow—but still focused and asks, "Who's out there?"

"I don't know. Could be Apaches, but they usually don't like to fight at night and likely would have already tried to steal the horses. After that, I really have no idea."

A plan starts to come into focus, but since we can't fight rifles with pistols, we're going to need Cisco's rifle. I hand Huck mine, get Cisco's attention and let them both know to lay down some fire so I can risk grabbing Cisco's Henry. As soon as they start shooting, I race to Cisco's gear, staying as low as possible and moving faster than I knew I could. I grab his Henry and practically fly back to the rocks and Huck.

Since Huck and I have the same rifle and it's better for him to have a gun he's familiar with, I let him keep my Winchester and I keep Cisco's Henry. I didn't have time to look for extra ammo, so all I've got is what's in the gun, and I'll need to make every shot count. I quickly check and am pleased to find the gun fully loaded, just like we've been talking about in our weekly practice sessions.

I'd rather Huck not draw any fire from our attackers unless it's absolutely necessary, so I tell him, "Huck, you don't shoot unless you are certain you can hit who you are shooting at"—I force a smile—"and that it's not me. But if they come close enough to camp that you can hit them, don't hesitate. Just like we've been practicing, take steady aim, don't rush and shoot for the chest. Once you start, keep shooting until you know they can't get up."

It's a terrible thing to have to say to a thirteen-year-old, but Huck has shown his toughness under fire before and we simply have no choice. He doesn't say a word, but I've come to know the look he just gave me, having first seen it last year when he wanted to go after three outlaws all by himself. It's a look of resolve, and I know Huck will do his best to do what needs to be done, as he always seems to. While I don't know who our attackers are or why they're attacking, they've made it clear they intend to kill all of us, and Huck's age isn't going to stop them.

There's a brief lull in the shooting, and I take the opportunity to slip back to my saddlebags, stick my second 1858 in my belt, grab my moccasins and quickly change out of my boots. Huck, glancing back, asks what I'm doing.

"I'm going to circle around and find out who's out there and how many there are."

I leave unsaid what I also plan to do when I find them, but Huck knows.

As I finish putting on my moccasins, Huck starts to turn toward me. "Huck, don't turn around. Keep your eyes and your attention forward until this is over." Probing shots are once again coming into camp, and while most are aimed at where Cisco is hidden, Huck needs to be focused on what's happening in front of him.

"I don't think there's too many of them out there, and I don't think they've done this much before, or we'd already be surrounded. Keep watching and remember not to look directly into the fire, or it will ruin your night vision. Keep listening to the shots. If they switch from rifles to pistols, that means they're getting closer to camp, so you do the same thing. Check now, before I go, and make sure your '49 is fully loaded. And every once in a while, slip your hand into your pocket to keep your fingers warm and ready. Unless you see someone, stay quiet and let Cisco do the shooting. I'll do what I can."

There is so much I want to say to Huck, so many things I want to tell him. He went through some very tough times last year, far more painful than a young boy should have to deal with. And now, still only thirteen years old, he finds himself in yet another gun battle. But there's no time to tell him how I'm feeling, though I hope he knows. The

11

only thing I can do is to try and keep him safe, to try and end this.

As shots continue to ring out, I do my best to suppress, or at least channel, my growing rage, knowing I need to focus completely. I look across at Cisco firing away, Frank dead by the fire, and my newly adopted son under attack. I have no idea who's attacking us, or why, but I no longer care. If any of them are left alive when I'm done, I'll ask then. But for now, my responsibility is to end this threat, and the best way to do that is to end their lives, which I fully intend to do.

I get Cisco's attention and motion for him to stay put and keep firing. He nods yes and watches me leave camp. Huck whispers good luck as I reach the trees. Choking back tears and anger, I can't respond, so I turn my attention forward and start moving toward where I believe our attackers are located.

I quickly cover about a hundred yards, trusting the moccasins, the deepening snow and the sound of gunfire to mask any noise, and I settle in behind a fallen tree. No shots are fired in my direction, so they don't know I'm here. The moon has come up enough in the past few minutes that when I peek over the tree, I can at least see shadows and outlines. The best I can tell, there appears to be four of them—and they're working their way forward toward our camp, toward Cisco and Huck.

From behind me, I can hear Cisco firing, and then I realize that some of the shots coming from our camp are too close together for them to all be from Cisco, so Huck must be firing as well. Huck's choice to ignore my orders fills me with a combination of frustration, fear and pride. But what it mostly does, now that they have to know where Huck is, is remove any hesitation about my next move. Now all I want to do is end this threat to me, to my friend and to my son. To do that, I need to kill these men.

I stay hidden on their left side as they continue to work their way forward. They're close enough that I can hear them talking, another sign of inexperience and overconfidence. Unfortunately, they're speaking Spanish, so I understand very little and not enough to be of any help. They're spaced out about ten yards apart. I focus on the one closest to me, not more than twenty-five yards away, as he unknowingly works his way toward me, firing blindly into our camp with no idea that I'm here. Not wanting to make any noise, I set the Henry down beside the tree, reach down to my right calf, pull out my Bowie knife and wait as he continues to draw closer. The Bowie is ten inches long and sharp enough to shave with. When I won it in a St. Louis poker game, it came with a wood handle, but I've since wrapped it tightly with leather, so it won't slip, just for times like this.

The four men are still talking to each other, not bothering to stay quiet as they get closer to our camp. The light dusting of snow I was expecting is quickly turning into a full storm. As cold as it is, the snow and wind does make my job easier. The closest man passes less than ten feet away from me, and as soon as he's past, I slide around the tree and sneak up behind him. I grab his face, and covering his mouth with my left hand, I reach up and, without hesitation, slit his throat with my right. As warm blood washes down my left arm, I hold him long enough to make sure he's dead—and he quickly is. I help him to the ground, out of concern for sound, not him, and watch his blood stain the gathering snow. I clean my Bowie in the snow, resheath it, take a couple steps back to the same tree and pick up the Henry.

I realize I was so focused on what I needed to do that I had blocked out all sound. But the voices are clear again, and one of the men, with increased urgency, is calling out for Javier, who will never answer again. This makes two things clear. One, I now know the name of the man I just killed, and two, they now know there is a problem, though I'm hoping they think Javier was hit by a shot from our camp. That hope is dashed when at least two of the men turn and start firing blindly toward where Javier was last seen—and where I am now. As hard as it is, I stay hidden and don't return fire, because this close, it wouldn't take a great shot—or even much luck—for three men with rifles to hit me, and I don't want them to know for sure that anyone is here.

Cisco and Huck must have figured out I'm under fire because they start pouring shots, even more rapidly, toward the remaining three men. I stay hidden behind the tree, not wanting to get hit by a stray shot, and soon the three men give up on me, turn their attention back toward camp and start moving forward. They draw closer together, another mistake of men inexperienced at this kind of work, and start to move more slowly, staying behind trees and rocks so as not to outline themselves against the growing moonlight. At this point, it is probably starting to sink in that they may no longer be the hunters, or at least not the only ones. Staying low, hoping not to draw attention from any of the remaining men, mine or theirs, I'm able to move from tree to tree until I am less than fifty feet away from the closest of the three remaining attackers.

I trade my rifle for my 1858 and, with no hesitation and two quick shots, drop a second attacker. The last two, seemingly more afraid of the unknown behind them than of whoever is in camp, both drop their rifles, grab their pistols and start moving quickly toward camp—and away from me. The one who is now closest to me heads toward where I know Huck is, but he's protected by rocks and trees and I can't get a decent shot off. The fourth one, the farthest away, is not as fortunate, and both Cisco and I have clear shots. We take them at almost the same time, and he drops, clearly dead.

As I race back toward camp, thinking only of Huck, all efforts at hiding forgotten, I hear shots, including the distinct sound of Huck's '49. Caution gone, I barrel into camp in time to see Cisco starting to come out from behind the tree and a man, clearly mortally wounded, but not yet dead, lying just outside of camp, slumped against a tree. I kick the gun out of his hand as I see Huck stand up from behind his rock. I can tell he's OK, or at least not wounded.

As I'm trying to figure out who this man is, and what—if anything—we should do for him, Cisco walks up, looks down and says, "Miguel."

Miguel looks at Cisco, then at me, and with surprise on his face says, "You're not wearing your hat." We all turn as Huck walks up, and Miguel, again with surprise on his face, and maybe a hint of irony in his voice, says, "I was killed by a boy." I look around and see that with all the trees in between where Cisco was hidden and where Miguel was shot, it couldn't have been Cisco who did it. But, from Huck's hiding place, it was a clear shot.

As this begins to sink in, Miguel fades away, and as he looks directly at me, fear in his eyes, his last word is, "Diego."

Three – Hattie's

Shortly after Ray and Sophie finished their dinner, Ray excused himself to join some of the other men who had already finished theirs and were gathered by the front door. Ray, along with Will and Thurm—and of course—Reverend Matt, had taken responsibility for building the new town church, the Dry Springs Church of the Resurrection. It was very close to being done, but it seemed that now, almost every day, new details had to be dealt with and the four of them were together almost any time they weren't working at their regular jobs. It made for long days, but they all felt it was worth it. For the good of the community, Thurm had financed most of the church, and the Rev (Dry Springs already had a Matt, so calling him Rev reduced confusion, and Reverend Matt liked it) had overseen the design, wanting the church to be beautiful, functional and welcoming to all faiths, or even those—and maybe especially those—who weren't sure of their faith. It came as a surprise to most of the townspeople, but Will had a special talent for woodworking, which he said he learned from his grandfather when he was a boy in Tennessee, and had made all of the pews by himself, with wood that Ray had paid for and had delivered from Denver.

For the past few months, while the new church was being built, Will had closed the Dusty Rose each Sunday morning and allowed it to serve as the temporary town church. If not unique, it was at least an unusual blending of God and bourbon. But the people of Dry Springs made it work. Sophie had once mentioned to Brock that she thought many of the women and children who came to church might be as much motivated by curiosity about what it was like inside a saloon—a place where they were normally not allowed—as they were by a desire to hear Reverend Matt's sermons.

At first, as soon as the Sunday services were over, Will would reopen the saloon, but since Christmas, he had taken to joining most of the townsfolk for dinner at Hattie's and then, surprisingly, taking the rest of the day off. When Ray asked Will once about closing on Sundays, he said, "Maybe it's some of Rev's words starting to sink in, or maybe it just doesn't seem right to go from a church to a saloon without a little more time in between. Or maybe, after working seven days a week my whole life, I'm getting tired and just need a day off, and Sunday seems like as a good a day as any. Any of these new people moving into town want to open a place and serve on Sundays, they're welcome to it. Town's growing so fast, maybe we need a second saloon anyway."

Sophie leaned back in her corner chair, comfortably alone at what had become her and Brock's regular Sunday table. She liked that she had a regular Sunday table, not just because Nolan and Nerissa ran such a nice restaurant, and not just because it gave her a break from preparing Sunday dinner, but also because after a whirlwind few months— which all started when Kurt and his men tried to take over Dry Springs and in many ways continued as more and more people moved into town—her life was starting to settle back into a comfortable pattern. With her wedding coming up in two weeks, the school having grown from the original seven children to more than twenty, and the challenges of learning how to be a mother to Huck keeping her busy, she hadn't had many quiet moments recently and was enjoying this one.

She missed Brock and Huck, but she knew they'd be home soon, maybe even tonight, so she took advantage of being alone and quietly watched the others as they enjoyed their Sunday dinner, and each other's company. Most would now be considered regulars, but it seemed like every week there were at least a couple of new faces. The town had almost tripled in size in the last few months, and there was no sign that it was going to slow down any time soon. Thurm said they now had over a thousand residents, counting the local farmers and ranchers who all shopped in Dry Springs. The article in the *Santa Fe New Mexican* newspaper about how the town had stood up for itself against Kurt and his gang of outlaws, prompted mainly by the heroics of Brock, had been picked up in papers around the country. It seemed to have struck quite a chord with people who were ready to leave where they were, but weren't sure where they wanted to go — until they heard about Dry Springs. It was good for the town to have such growth, but it naturally led to changes, and everyone, new and old, were still learning and adjusting.

Without Sophie having to say a word, Nerissa brought her a second cup of tea, shared a tired, friendly smile and whispered, "I love that Hattie's is so busy, but with these crowds, especially when the McClaskey's join us, Sundays seem just a little longer than most days. I don't know if it's the end of a long week or the start of a new one, but once we close up and I get Oscar and Hattie off to bed, I'm ready to sleep for a week."

While everyone raved about Nolan's pot roast and stood in line for Nerissa's baked goods, especially the donuts, Sophie thought that other than the company, the tea was the highlight of Hattie's. Nerissa had it shipped over from London to Denver, and from there it came to Dry Springs in the increasingly frequent deliveries of goods from Denver. It was expensive, but a small indulgence that Sophie loved and allowed herself.

Sophie looked around again at how beautiful Hattie's had turned out. Nolan and Nerissa had a great relationship with Ansel and Dorothy Portis, and having Hattie's as a part of their Soft Beds Hotel was working out well for everyone. At the rate Dry Springs was growing, there would have to be another hotel built soon, and it would be great for the Soft Beds' business to have Hattie's as a regular draw. Being located directly across the street from the Dusty Rose didn't hurt either, as many a farmer and cowboy, after a hard night of drinking and gambling, thought it was much more convenient to walk across the street and get a room than it was to ride out in the middle of the night, sometimes quite a few miles, to their ranch or farm. It also didn't hurt knowing that when they woke up, some of Nerissa's now famous donuts would be waiting for them, fresh out of the oven.

Shawn and Kim usually had Sunday dinner with Matt and Stacy. But, with Matt working on the church and Stacy home taking care of her dog, Gus, who'd broken his leg in a fight with a coyote, they were eating by themselves. Shawn had recently finished building his blacksmith shop, adding an extension to what was formerly known as Parker's Livery and is now known as Huck & Dixon's Blacksmith & Livery. The name was already so long that they didn't add to it, but Shawn also did gunsmith work and had quickly developed a reputation throughout the territory as a man with a magic touch with any kind of weapon. And since Shawn and Kim didn't mind pitching in with the livery side of the business when Huck and Tom were in school, they didn't have to pay any rent.

Right up front, taking up almost a quarter of the entire restaurant, were the McClaskeys, big and little, for a total of thirteen—including Mrs. and Mrs. and all nine of their combined children—big-eating, big-voiced, lovable McClaskeys. They only came to church about once a month, but when they did, they always came to Hattie's afterwards. Knowing how much space they took up and how much food they ate, the mothers McClaskey always stopped by on their way to church to let Nolan and Nerissa know that they were going to need plenty of extra pot roast and mashed potatoes and at least three of Nerissa's apple pies.

Cat, Maria, baby Enyeto and Clybs were wrapping up their meal a couple of tables away from Sophie. Even though he wasn't yet twenty years old, Brock had made Clybs his deputy, and Clybs loved the role. Sophie thought he also loved Cat, but wasn't sure that Cat felt the same way, though she was always friendly. Enyeto, who only recently had learned to walk, was stretching his little legs as well as the patience of Maria. Cat packed up the balance of their meals in a bag Nerissa brought to the table, while Maria tracked Enyeto down.

Maria and Cat, having finished as much of their meal as baby Enyeto was going to allow, paid their bill and waved goodbye to Nerissa. Since Maria and Cisco were getting married at the same time as Sophie and Brock, they had plenty to talk about, and Sophie thought this morning would be a great time to go over some of the details, especially about the dress that Maria was making her. On her way out, Sophie's attention was drawn to a man, eating alone, who was new to town, but looked vaguely familiar. She took a second look, but then, thinking about her wedding dress, she forgot about the man and hurried to catch Maria.

Four - Brock

I look around and can't find any evidence that there is anyone out there beyond the four we've killed. I can hear their horses whinnying off in the distance. It's a strangely lonely sound, almost as if they know something has happened and aren't sure what their future holds. But maybe that's just me. Huck is looking down and slowly reloading his '49 Colt. I wonder how hard this is going to be on him. I wish there was time to deal with that right now, but there isn't. Cisco is staring at Miguel, crossing himself and mouthing words that I'm guessing are a prayer. I'm not too sure about heaven and hell, even though I've been listening to Reverend Matt every Sunday, but if they do exist, I wouldn't want to be in Miguel's boots right now.

Talking as much to himself as he is to Huck and me, Cisco whispers, "I knew him. He worked for Chavez. He was the foreman. He came in when Chavez brought in the cattle a couple of years ago. I didn't think he was a gunman."

I'm not feeling too generous toward the men who killed Frank and tried to kill the rest of us, and looking down at Miguel—who is now partially covered in snow, his eyes frozen wide open, and maybe dealing with the eternal consequences of his actions—I say, as much as to him as to Cisco and Huck, "Looks like he should have stuck to cattle."

Miguel's comment about my hat is nagging at me, but their isn't the time to try and figure it out. I do remember Diego as Chavez's gun hand, and while the last time I saw him we didn't part on the best of terms, there wasn't enough bad blood there to cause him to send four men after me. Plus, Diego had struck me as a man who wouldn't hire others to do his killing. He had enough confidence in his ability and enough mean in his personality that if he wanted you dead he'd want to do it himself and watch you die. So, while I don't know yet why this is happening, or even what is happening, the odds are it's not over yet.

"Huck, you go bring in their horses." I reach down and pick Miguel's gun out of the blood-soaked snow, toss it to Cisco and tell him, "Start digging a grave for Frank. Make it close to the fire—the ground should be thawed a bit there. I'm going back for your Henry and the rest of their weapons."

"What about burying the others?" asks Cisco.

I think about it for a moment, knowing Huck's going to hear—and learn from—what I have to say, but deciding that that's OK. "Cisco, unless one of these men was a friend of yours and you feel we should, I'm not inclined to spend the next few hours digging graves out of the frozen ground for the men who killed Frank—and tried to kill us. I know burying them is the decent thing to do, but these weren't decent men."

Without knowing who the other three men were, Cisco looks at Huck, then me, and says, "No, these men were not my friends." With one last look at Miguel, he turns and walks back to the fire, which is still going strong enough to remind me that all of this took place in a few short minutes. Cisco turns away from the now burning antelope steaks and the boiling coffee, grabs his small camp shovel and starts one of the worst jobs any man can do—digging a grave for a friend.

As Huck leaves to find their horses and bring them back to camp, I walk over to my gear, stow my second 1858 and trade my moccasins for my boots, the need to be silent gone, though it is eerily quiet as the three of us are lost in our own thoughts and the now heavy snow muffles all sounds.

24

It only takes a couple of minutes to pick up the weapons from Javier and the other two, as well as grab the Henry. I bring them all back to camp, giving my rifle a quick cleaning, loading it back into its scabbard and setting the others in a pile on the blanket where Cisco set Miguel's pistol. I turn around to go help Huck, but he's already walking back to camp, leading three horses in. He looks at me with tears flowing down his face.

"One of them musta got hit by a stray bullet. She was dead when I found 'em."

I remember back to last year and the first day I rode into Dry Springs, when the first person I met was Huck. He was working at his dad's livery, and it was clear even then how much he loved horses. I think his favorite part of most days is still when he's down at the livery, working with his best friend Tom and the horses, especially Spirit. Or maybe it's when he's out riding Spirit, but either way, it almost certainly involves horses. And now, on top of knowing he killed Miguel, he realizes he may very well have shot a horse, and even if it was done accidently, it's eating away at him.

Just as I did last year, following all of the trouble with his dad and Kurt's gang, I find myself asking how much one young boy can take. I walk toward him.

"Huck…"

He looks at me. "Let me take care of these horses while you and Cisco take care of Frank." He keeps walking toward Horse and Spirit, the three horses following obediently behind. As he walks by, my heart filled with awe and sadness, I notice none of the horses have brands, which is surprising. As valuable and important as horses are in the

West, you don't see many unbranded horses, which has me thinking that these boys wanted their identity to remain a secret. And it would have, if we'd all been killed or, since we weren't, if Cisco hadn't been here to recognize Miguel.

As Cisco keeps digging Frank's grave, I start to go through his stuff. I don't find anything in his pockets, except his pipe and some tobacco. I set that, along with his pistol, on the blanket with the Chavez men's weapons and start to go through the rest of Frank's gear. The only thing I find that you wouldn't find in almost any man's trail gear is a letter.

The envelope is addressed to Frank Sierra, and the return address is from Guatemala. All I know about Guatemala is that it's somewhere below Mexico. I don't remember Frank ever mentioning it. I realize as I'm looking at the letter how little I know about him. I didn't even know his last name was Sierra. He fought with us in the battle against Kurt and his men and he lived outside of town, though I've never been to his place. And he made his money working for farmers and ranchers in the area. He'd hire himself out during planting season, or when it was time to round up someone's cattle, and he was known as a good hand, always friendly, and always willing to work. Kept to himself mostly, though we'd shared a few beers at the Dusty Rose. He was as happy buying a round as he was having one bought for him. He'd spent some time working on the new church, always declining Thurm's offers to pay him, just happy to pitch in.

I open the letter and it's in Spanish, which means I can't read a word. "Cisco, how about I dig for a while and you read this letter I found in Frank's stuff? Maybe we can learn something about him. Huck, you clean our weapons and make sure they're all fully loaded and ready to go."

Cisco steps out of the deepening grave, and I trade the letter for the shovel, thinking I have the easier job. Huck, having finished with the Chavez horses, moves closer to the fire, warms his hands and gets to work on the guns. Cisco moves closer to the fire too, for warmth and light. He sits down and gently slips the letter out of the worn envelope, holding it for a moment before opening it, his head dipped in sadness or maybe out of respect for Frank—probably both. Huck looks at me, and we're both quiet until Frank slowly opens the letter and begins to softly read.

Dearest Paco,

I hope you are well in America. I must tell you the worst news. Papa has died. Just like when we were kids, he was still the first one in the fields every day, and that is where I found him. He died working the plow, fighting the bad weather and the dying crops. We still do not have any rain. I think Papa's heart gave out after all these years. We buried him next to the field so that he can still look over and protect us. I think he would have liked that. Everyone from town came for the funeral and many nice things were said about Papa. Mama is OK, but she doesn't talk much anymore, always looking away at things I can't see. I think she will join him soon. Maybe that is good.

The money you send is welcome and gives us food, which we need. Thank you. But every day, even though it's been almost ten years, Mama asks when you are coming home. With Papa dead, you are the oldest, and maybe it is time to come home? Maylin had a baby girl, so now, without you, we are twelve.

Please write soon and tell us more about your town and maybe tell us you are coming home. Mama and everyone love you.

Your brother,

Fredy

Cisco sits for a moment before folding the letter and putting it carefully back in the envelope. I realize I've stopped digging. "Huck, when we get home, you sell the Chavez horses and Frank's horse. I'll ask your grandpa to sell the guns we took from these men, as well as Frank's gun." I turn to Cisco. "Can you write in Spanish?"

"Si."

"Will you write a letter to his brother and explain what happened? Tell him things about Frank—how he fought in the war, how he fought for the town, how hard he worked and how everyone liked him. We'll take the money from the horses and the weapons and send it with the letter. When we get back, I'll ask Thurm if Frank owned the property he lived on, and if he did, we'll sell that too."

Without a word, they both signal their agreement, and I turn back to my digging. No one says anything, but we all know we aren't staying here for the night, and Cisco starts to pack up camp while Huck finishes up with the guns. With each of us lost in our own thoughts, the silence descends again, like a heavy blanket, with even the sounds of our working muted by the deepening snow.

I finish the grave about the same time Cisco and Huck finish packing up, with Huck having done my gear and Cisco having done Frank's. Cisco and I lift Frank and set him gently into the grave while Huck grabs the shovel and starts to cover him. I reach for the shovel, but Huck holds on, says he wants to do it. I think Huck might be burying more than Frank, so I let him keep the shovel and find things to do around camp to give him some privacy. Probably sensing the same thing, Cisco says he'll go do one last check and make sure we didn't miss anything where the three men who died outside camp still lie.

After a while, Huck's about done and Cisco and I drift back to the fire and the grave. To protect Frank's grave from the coyotes, we cover it with heavy rocks, hoping the coyotes will be deterred by the rocks and satisfied with the four men scattered dead around camp. We stand quietly for a moment, and Cisco says, "When I knew him, he seemed like a good man." He crosses himself and we all walk to our horses. I take the lead and Huck follows, with our pack horses, Frank's horse, and the three Chavez horses strung out behind him. Cisco takes up the rear.

Without looking back, we head out toward Dry Springs.

Five - Wolf

The men were moving slowly, and Wolf walked alongside the smaller man, as she had been doing for the past week. She had recently taken to walking close to—or even on—the trail, often in plain sight of those who traveled with the smaller man, something she had never done before. She was fully alert, and if she sensed danger, she could still disappear from the trail in an instant and become invisible in a moment. But for now, she stayed closer to the smaller man than she ever had the other one, even sleeping close to him and, on rare occasions, allowing him to touch her.

Wolf was still adjusting to her new life, which for the past few months rarely included the men traveling. The smaller man, if alone, would sometimes share his food with her, which was new, but she enjoyed it. In the last few weeks, though no one knew it, not even the small man, she had slept under the back porch of the house.

Because the men didn't travel as much as they had when it was just her and the larger man, and because Wolf still had the urge to roam, she would sometimes take off for days at a time, trusting the men would be there when she returned and knowing the smaller man trusted that she would return.

Her instincts told her they were heading back to where they stayed most of the time, and she didn't sense any danger on the trail. So, as they worked their way back to Dry Springs, Wolf settled into an easy walk, looking up occasionally at the small man.

Scott Harris

Six - Brock

The steady snow blocks out most of the light the moon might have given us, so we ride slowly, our horses unsure of their footing. We've only ridden for about an hour, driven by a need to get away from what we left behind and to get closer to home. I don't know how long it will take, but an hour certainly hasn't been long enough to shake the image of Frank lying lifeless in the snow. By now, the coyotes have almost certainly started their work on the four men left unburied, and if there's anything left in the morning, the vultures will make sure those men will soon be nothing more than a memory—and a bad one at that.

Nobody is talking as we're all lost in our own thoughts. I have to fight the urge to think about Huck and what this night will mean to him, to us, to Sophie. As important as that is, I know I need to focus my attention on trying to figure out what happened and maybe even why. I keep coming back to Miguel's comment, "You're not wearing your hat," and remembering how all of the first shots were at Frank, though with four of them—and the advantage of complete surprise—they could have shot any of us or, if they were decent shots, all of us. It takes me a bit, but I finally realize and accept that their real target was me, which makes Frank's death even sadder, and me even angrier.

While never intentionally, I have managed to accumulate some enemies over the last couple of years, and if, for reasons I don't understand or am not aware of, one or some of them were driven to try and track me down and kill me, that's unfortunately part of the life I have been leading. But Frank? To the best of my knowledge, he didn't have an enemy in the world, and certainly not in Dry Springs. Frank died because evil men exist and they often don't mind killing and, mostly, because he was mistaken for me. At first, I might have been able to attribute this to a vicious robbery gone wrong. Maybe bad luck on our part and cruel desperation on theirs. But not with Miguel's hat comment and certainly not with his last word—Diego—which felt like a threat, or a warning, or maybe both.

It seems clear now that Chavez is involved in this, but I can't figure out why. I didn't part the best of friends with him or his hired gun Diego, but looking back on what happened down in Tesuque on Chavez's cattle ranch, it doesn't make sense that months later he would send four of his men to kill me. For what? Pride? Honor? Money? When Cisco, Maria and the others left Tesuque, they took only what could fit in a small wagon, which was very little, and left behind everything else they had ever known, and even that was still very little. And that last day, when Chavez left our traveling group and turned back down Coyote Creek toward his beautiful home and spectacular ranch, Cisco rode with him for a couple of hours and came back feeling that everything between them was forgiven and buried.

But, for reasons I'll need to figure out, it appears the only thing buried is Frank.

My mind drifts to the four men who killed Frank, the men we killed. I wonder if they have families back home, people who are waiting for them, like Sophie is waiting for Huck and me, or Maria is waiting for Cisco. People who will grow more and more anxious with time and eventually come to accept that the men they're waiting for are not coming home, ever. If they had wives and children, did these men imagine as they said goodbye and rode away toward Dry Springs that they'd never see them again? That they'd leave them alone and unprotected in a harsh world? Did they have letters in their saddlebags that will never be answered?

While I have no doubt that each of them got exactly what they deserved, I can't help but think that there are others out there who will be hurt by the decisions they made. Are men who kill for money and greed ever haunted with these same questions?

Knowing I'll never have answers, I turn my attention to finding a place to set up camp. Only a few minutes later, we ride into a spot that will work well for the night. There's a large rock overhang, almost a shallow cave, that looks like it has room for the three of us. The nearby trees are thick and will provide some shelter for all of the horses. There's no water, at least not close by, but we have our full canteens and can melt snow for the horses. There is grass for the horses to roll in and enough for them to eat their fill.

Huck and Cisco close up behind me, and without a word we all dismount. Cisco immediately starts gathering wood for a fire, and Huck and I look to the horses.

Unfortunately, we only have enough blankets for the horses we started with, not for the three from the killers. We find a couple of large trees that offer some protection from the wind and snow and picket them a little closer to each other than we normally would, hoping that will provide them some warmth. As usual, we don't picket Horse and Spirit, but, not surprisingly, they quickly find comfort and warmth with the others and stay close to them.

Cisco gets a fire started, banking it up against the rocks and as far back underneath the overhang as he can get. It offers some protection from the growing cold, a strong fire often having as much impact on the soul as it does on the body. Even though we didn't get to eat earlier, none of us are hungry now, and Cisco skips the antelope steaks and just gets the coffee going. Normally the smell of coffee on a freezing night is one of the great smells and one of the great medicines for men on the trail. But tonight, it just doesn't seem like quite enough. I walk over to our gear, slip a flask out of my saddlebag and add a bit of bourbon to our mugs, even a little for Huck. It's another one of those things I'll have to talk to Sophie about, but if I'm being honest with myself, it's only to share with her, not to ask if it's OK. I'm still trying to figure out how to be a dad, but some things just seem right and this is one of them. Huck nods and takes a sip, and when he doesn't react at all to the strong taste of bourbon, I'm reminded of the time he spends with Ray and the rules I know they break together. On occasion, bourbon must be one of them.

We settle down around the fire, and the quiet, while not uncomfortable, is still there. I light up a cigar, but without taking my time as I usually do when sitting around a campfire. Wolf appears, so quickly and quietly I wonder if she's been there the whole time. She comes closer to the fire, and to Huck, than I can remember her doing before. She settles into the snow, facing Huck and the fire, her thick fur protecting her from the cold.

I know Huck has a lot of thinking to do and we have quite a few conversations coming up about what happened tonight. Even with everything he went through last year—being beaten by outlaws, witnessing killings, burying his own father, and living alone until Sophie and I took him in—up until tonight, he has never killed a man. And Cisco, who up until last year when I found him pinned down by thieves who had already killed his best friend and were trying to kill him, had never even been in a fistfight, much less a gunfight, will have to start dealing with having killed a man tonight, no matter how justified it was.

These are tough things for good men to deal with. And then I realize. Huck, who has only been a part of my life, has only been my son, for the last few months, is no longer a boy. With everything he has been through, with the way he has handled things, it is unfair to think of him as anything but a man. You don't have to have been through what Huck has been through—and you certainly don't have to have killed a man—in order be a man. But you can't have gone through and seen and done those things and stand tall like Huck is doing, without being a man.

Watching Cisco and Huck, I find my mind drifting back to London. I loved being raised by my mom and my uncle, but I realize now how isolated I was. I didn't have any brothers or sisters, and I didn't have any true friends, not in the way that Huck has Tom, or—and it hits me for the first time—I now have Cisco and some of the other men in town. Even my first couple of years in America, while I met quite a few people—and spent some time with many of them—I would struggle to remember most of their names. And now I have a family and good friends. People whom I wouldn't hesitate to risk my life to protect and who would—and have—done the same for me.

My uncle trained me to be able to defend myself, with my brains, my fists or a gun. But because of where and how we lived, I never really needed those skills until I moved to America. And now I need them on a regular basis, far more than I could have ever imagined when I boarded that ship in London, and far more than I would like. The life I'm leading is nothing like the life I led in London or expected to live while visiting America. But, I'm suddenly struck by a thought: I'm no longer visiting—this is my life. I realize it's been a while since anyone has commented on my British accent, something that happened all the time when I first arrived in America. I wonder if I even have an accent anymore. If I visited London, would I stand out now? Would I be the one who speaks funny?

And then I realize I'm not going back to London. I came here looking for my father, knowing I would eventually be heading back home to the life I knew and the people I love. But I now know this is my home, and while I love and miss my mom and my uncle, these are my people and this is my family.

And this is where I wish Sophie were here. Having grown up in tiny Dry Springs—and having rarely left, never going farther than Denver—she is somehow much more worldly than I am. When things move beyond the simple for me, she has a way of clarifying things, helping me understand them. And tonight, I need her. Maybe that's what marriage is.

As I'm thinking about that, the silence is broken by Huck, who's decided it's time to talk about what happened tonight.

"What did Miguel mean when he said, "You're not wearing your hat?""

Seven - Brock

As I'm struggling to find the best way to answer Huck's question, knowing this is another of those conversations that will stay with Huck—and with me—for a long time, Cisco jumps right in.

"It means they were trying to kill your dad."

I'm not sure I would have been that blunt, but I guess there is no other way to answer the question. Huck looks at me for a moment, but without the surprise that I expected. He turns back to Cisco, who continues to explain.

"They knew about the hat, and when they saw Frank wearing it, they thought he was your dad. So, they killed him. They were going to kill the rest of us to keep us quiet, or to be sure they had gotten your dad, or maybe both."

I take a sip of my bourboned coffee, watching Huck and, if I'm honest with myself, relieved that Cisco has been the one to explain to Huck what happened. I watch as a couple of snowflakes drift into my mug and melt instantly. The only sound I can hear, other than the horses softly whinnying to each other, is the fire crackling. I look up at Huck, but he's still looking at Cisco, knowing there is more.

"Are you sure?"

"Yes, Huck, I am. There is no reason for them to know anything about what kind of hat your dad wears unless they were looking for him." They both look at me or, rather, at my hat, which, as stubborn as I am, I now know I'll be wearing for as long as it holds out.

"Those men had no reason to be here, so far from Mr. Chavez's ranch. I knew Miguel from the ranch, and while I didn't see the other men, they either worked on the ranch or were hired for this job. I don't remember Miguel ever leaving the ranch before. The surprise he showed when he saw your dad was still alive tells us why they came, and when he said "Diego," it meant this isn't done."

Huck asks, "Who's Diego?"

I jump in. "Huck, do you remember Black?" He nods yes.

"Cisco, you've heard us talk about Kurt and what happened when I first came to Dry Springs."

"Sí."

"Black was Kurt's enforcer, and other than Kurt, he was the top gun in the gang. In all the time you worked for Chavez, did you ever see Diego do any work? Do anything other than always be at Chavez's side?"

"No."

"That's because his only job was to protect Chavez and do his gun bidding. Miguel, who was clearly afraid of Diego, knew that if they failed to kill me, Chavez would send Diego to do the job. When did Diego first start working for Chavez?"

"He showed up shortly after Mr. Chavez switched from sheep to cattle."

"I've been thinking about this since we started riding tonight. Things didn't seem quite right with Chavez, even before he tried to steal your money. I remember when I was in Santa Fe the men were talking about how, for the past few months, he'd been doing more gambling than ever before, not just in Santa Fe, but in Tucson and Denver, and was losing a lot of money. I think Chavez has gotten himself into some serious financial trouble, and when it started, he got scared and brought in Diego for protection. Even if I'm right, and I'm pretty sure I am, I still don't know how that would lead to what happened tonight, or to what I think is going to happen once he figures out Miguel and those other boys failed. But you're right, Cisco—I'm afraid this isn't over."

I let that sink in, as much for me as for Huck and Cisco. I have to start accepting that for whatever reason, I am now a hunted man. That's never good news, but now it's not just me. I have Sophie and Huck to think about, and after what happened tonight, it's clear that others around me are in danger too.

"Huck, we've never really talked about why Cisco and the others moved to Dry Springs. Cisco, OK if I tell him?"

"Of course."

"You know the story of me finding Cisco under attack in Coyote Creek and how we were both saved by Delgadito and the other Muache Indians. How when it was over, Delgadito gave Cisco the gift of Regalo. What I never told you, was how when Cisco and I made it back to the ranch he worked for, Francisco Chavez's Rancho del Cielo, Chavez tried to steal Cisco and Maria's money. Together, we were able to get their money back and keep whatever belongings they could fit into their wagon, but Cisco was forced to leave behind the only job, the only home—the only life—he had ever known. On the trip home to Dry Springs is

41

when we fought the Apaches and when Cisco's brother, Danny, was killed."

Huck looks over at Cisco, and I realize they share something that I can't fully understand, each having suffered terrible losses and had their entire lives uprooted by events they couldn't control and for reasons they can't understand.

"When we left Chavez's ranch, I was concerned that he would send men after us, as much for pride as for the money or whatever small belongings Cisco and his family had taken with them. We had to move slowly because we had the wagon and because Maria was with child, though she lost the baby on the trip back. We would have been easy to trail, and it wouldn't have taken many men to wipe us out. To make sure we weren't followed and attacked, I forced Chavez to ride with us for a while. He tried to bring Diego along, but I wouldn't allow it. Neither Chavez nor Diego was happy about it, but there really wasn't much they could do, short of a gunfight. Chavez was true to his word—we weren't followed. And I thought, apparently incorrectly, that was the end of it."

We all take a quiet minute to think about what this means. Chavez has plenty of resources to call on, and sending four men tonight means that for reasons not yet known to us, he's serious and this isn't going to end tonight. The snow starts coming down harder, and the wind seems to be picking up again. It feels like it's getting even colder. I button my coat up tight, move closer to the fire and freshen up my coffee, both from the pot and the flask. Cisco does the same. Huck warms up his coffee, but I shake my head no when he looks at the flask.

"Once we felt safe, I allowed Chavez to go back to his ranch, and Cisco rode with him for a while. Cisco, when

42

you got back from your ride with Chavez, other than saying everything was OK, you never said what you talked about. You just said we didn't have to worry anymore. I didn't want to pry, but now I'm wondering…"

Cisco looks away from Huck and to me. "I will tell you what I remember, though I don't know if it will help.

"He didn't say anything at first, and so we rode the first few miles in silence. He didn't look at me, or at anything. His eyes were down, and we just rode in the middle of Ciyote Creek, heading back in the direction of his ranch. Eventually he started talking, but he still didn't look at me. I'm not even sure he was talking to me. It almost seemed like he was talking to himself. He said he was sorry about what happened to P'oe and to the rest of us, but he never apologized for what he did. It's like he was talking about someone else.

"He mumbled that things weren't going right and he had to figure out what to do. I still wasn't sure he was talking to me, as much as he was to himself, so I still didn't say anything. So many bad things had happened in that creek in the past week, I was happy not to have to talk so I could watch for trouble. We kept riding, and even though he kept talking, he kept getting quieter and quieter and finally, I couldn't understand anymore what he was saying. Suddenly, after not talking at all for a while, he shook his head, looked up and seemed surprised to see me. He reached out, shook my hand and wished me good luck. He put the spurs to his horse and was gone without another word. I watched until he was out of sight, then turned back and caught up with everyone else. I didn't think I'd ever see him again, so I didn't think much about it. Until tonight."

I kind of wish Cisco had told me then, but I don't know that I would have done anything different. It does seem to confirm that Chavez has real troubles, and like many a man who is in danger of losing what he has, especially his pride, he had started to make some bad decisions. While I understand that, after what happened tonight, he's lost any chance of gaining my sympathy. And while I wonder why he's doing what he's doing, I'm far more concerned with what he's going to do. I don't know how long ago those men left to track me down, but even riding hard, it's a few days ride from Chavez's ranch to Dry Springs, so I figure it will be a while before Chavez realizes they aren't coming back. That gives me a little bit of time to try and figure out what to do.

Huck, who appears to take all of this in stride and seems to be afraid of nothing, asks, "What are we going to do?"

"For now? Nothing. We're going to try and get a good night's sleep, get back home tomorrow and then figure out what needs to be done."

Knowing he's not happy with the answer, but not knowing what else to tell him—or Sophie—I shake off the snow, walk over to our gear and bring back all three bedrolls. We set up pretty close to the fire, happy to all fit under the overhang. Trusting Wolf and Horse to let us know if someone gets close, we settle down, each silently reflecting on the day. Trying to put aside, just for a little while, what's happened and what this all will mean to Huck, I turn my thoughts toward home—and Sophie. And for the first time tonight, just a little, I smile.

Eight - Sophie

Sophie and her dad had enjoyed a nice evening meal, and now the kitchen was clean, her lessons for school tomorrow were ready, and Ray, tired from a long weekend of working on the church, had excused himself and gone to bed early. Sophie debated for a moment between going to bed early herself, settling into a warm, comfortable chair with a book, or, as she ultimately decided to do, pour herself a glass of bourbon and sit outside on the front porch.

Between her job as a teacher, Brock's job as town sheriff, raising Huck and planning for the wedding, quiet nights on the porch were few and far between. But when they did happen, they might have been some of her favorite times. She looked across at Brock's empty chair and wondered again where he and Huck were and if they were safe. There was no reason to think they weren't, but knowing that anything can happen when traveling in the territory and being a bit disappointed they weren't home yet, she had just a little nagging feeling in the pit of her stomach she couldn't shake.

The wind had picked up in the late afternoon, but it was blowing in from behind the house, so she was protected from most of it. The snow was coming down harder, but the cover over the porch kept her almost snow free. The penetrating cold was still there, though and she hoped that Brock and Huck were warm. She took another look back through the window at the roaring fire and the enticing soft leather chair in the living room, but decided to stay outside anyway. She buttoned her coat up all the way and pulled her knit cap down over her ears. She was wearing one of Brock's flannel shirts under her coat, the comfort coming as much from the familiar smell as from the warmth it provided.

She'd first worn one of Brock's shirts when she'd had to step outside one chilly morning, for only a minute, and it had been hanging conveniently on a peg by the front door. She liked the way it felt and smelled and now she found herself wearing one most of the evenings when he worked late and every day since he and Huck had been gone on this trip.

No doubt the bourbon also helped to take the edge off of the cold. Since the girls, Nerissa, Maria and Kim, had moved into town, Sophie had taken to drinking sherry, something she had never tried before they moved here. But the girls had fallen into the habit of getting together almost every Thursday evening to enjoy a glass (or two) of sherry, some good conversation and each other's company. Recently, Maria's sister Cat had started joining the girls, meaning the group had outgrown their regular meeting place, Sophie's living room. So now they met at Hattie's, after Nerissa closed up for the day. Sometimes, if any of the girls got there a little early, they helped Nerissa close up and clean up, which somehow was much more fun when doing it for someone else than it was at home.

The gatherings were a weekly highlight for Sophie, and enjoying sherry had spilled over to her time at home with Brock. But when Brock was gone, she found herself shifting back to a bit of bourbon, which somehow, like wearing his shirt, made her feel closer to him.

Her mind drifted to their wedding, and it struck her that two weeks from right now, she would be married. She wondered what changes that would bring, not just for her, but for all of them. The most obvious was that Brock would be changing bedrooms, moving from the one he shared with Huck to the one they had built for themselves as an extension on her dad's house. She was naturally nervous and excited about that, but knew it would be good. Excluding the bedroom, they had been living as she thought a married couple would for the past few months, so she wasn't sure what, if any, additional changes there would be. Still, the wedding felt to Sophie as if it would bring a permanence to the relationship, something she hadn't known she wanted until Brock had asked her to marry him—which she was still grateful for every day.

Sophie was excited about sharing the day with Cisco and Maria. She had only known them for a few months, but it was obvious from the start that they loved each other, and it seemed that Cisco was the only one in town who was surprised when they became engaged. After all of the tragedy they suffered—Maria losing her baby and her husband P'oe, who was also Cisco's best friend, and then Cisco's brother Danny being killed—it was good for Sophie, and the entire town, to watch them find happiness with each other. Those who watched Cisco with baby Enyeto often commented that he couldn't treat him any better if he had been his own.

The new church was beautiful. Thurm had surprised many when, with his own money, he ordered stained glass from New York, an extravagance that most small towns didn't enjoy but one that added so much to the beauty of the Dry Springs Church of the Resurrection. The thick walls would help keep the church warm in the winter and cool in the summer, and Will had crafted enough hardwood pews to seat a hundred people. There was room to add more, too, as the town, and the church, grew. Sophie knew that Reverend Matt had been working for the past few weeks on his first sermon in the new church, and with the weddings taking place later that same afternoon, it was a perfect way to open the new church.

Everyone in town was looking forward to it, large weddings being fairly uncommon in Dry Springs and double weddings unheard of. But the four of them had grown to be close friends and were all happy to share the day, and because of economic realities, it made good sense to do so.

It was looking like the biggest day in Dry Springs history, with the exception of the day Kurt and his gang were wiped out. Thurm and the others were rushing to finish the church. Nerissa was making not one, but two, wedding cakes—one chocolate and one vanilla. And dispensing with traditional invitations, the entire town had been invited. Every business planned on closing that Sunday, and it promised to be a perfect day.

Sophie thought about how much she missed her mom and how she would have wanted her to be there for the wedding, and all of the things leading up to it. She found herself wondering what her mom would have thought of Brock, and Huck. But in her heart, she knew she'd have loved them. Sophie was drifting in that place somewhere between lost in thought and dozing off, when she heard a small voice.

She looked up and saw Maria standing there, asking, for the second time, "Sophie, are you awake?"

Sophie stood up, surprised she hadn't noticed Maria making the almost half mile walk from town to the house, all of it over open ground, and said, "Hello, Maria. Sorry, I didn't see you walking up. I was thinking about my mom, and the boys, and I guess I dozed off. Is everything OK?"

Smiling, Maria answered, "Yes, thank you. Enyeto is asleep and Cat is with him. I felt like taking a walk, and it led me here. I've been thinking a lot about Cisco tonight."

"I'm sure they're fine. I'm guessing, or hoping, they'll be home tomorrow. Can I get you a cup of coffee, or maybe a glass of sherry?"

With a beautiful, mischievous smile that Sophie had come to love, Maria answered, "Maybe both?"

They walked into the house, Sophie moving toward the sherry, and Maria, with the familiarity of a good friend, helping herself to a cup of coffee. With a mother's intuition, sensing that someone was asleep, Maria dropped her voice to a whisper. "I thought they might have been home tonight."

Sophie finished pouring Maria a glass, nodded her agreement and headed back out to the front porch. Maria helped herself to a little cream for her coffee and joined her, taking Brock's chair.

"That's what I was thinking about, or maybe dreaming about, when you walked up. Brock hasn't been gone all that much the last few months, and I guess I've gotten used to him being here. And this time he has Huck with him, and I'm really not used to that, though I guess I'll have to start getting used it."

Maria nodded slowly, took a sip of her sherry and quietly responded, "After what happened to P'oe and Danny, I'm not sure I'll ever be OK with Cisco being gone, but I didn't want to say anything to him. He was so excited about this trip, seeing his Indian friends and hunting ... It's just that I won't feel right, I won't feel safe, until he's back."

The girls sat quietly for a couple of minutes, comfortable with the silence in the way only good friends can be, both thinking about their husbands-to-be and, in Sophie's case, about Huck.

Maria broke the silence. "The dresses are almost ready."

Maria was sewing both of the wedding dresses. Though she'd been sewing her entire life, neither she nor Sophie knew much at all about current fashion, and they knew almost nothing about wedding dresses. But with Stacy and Kim helping out by sharing their dresses and their experiences, plus some pictures cut out of magazines Nerissa had sent down from Denver, the dresses were turning out to be beautiful. Maria had made hers in the traditional Mexican huipil style, and Sophie's was an ivory-colored, lace, two-piece dress that was already more beautiful than anything she could have imagined.

The girls had talked before about how much they would have loved to have their moms at the wedding, but like Sophie's mom, Maria's had passed away. Sophie felt fortunate that her dad was able to be there and was going to give her away. Ray had been honored when Maria, who had also lost her father, asked him to give her away too. With Cisco and Maria working for Ray at Hinton's General Store, they had grown close to Ray these past couple of months, but Ray was still surprised—and pleased—when Maria asked.

To many in town, it seemed like the perfect way to break in the new church. The town's first inhabitant, Ray, giving away his daughter and, at the same time, giving away one of the newest members of the Dry Springs community.

Sophie thanked Maria for probably the tenth time for making the dress, and the girls talked for almost an hour, having a couple more cups of hot coffee once the sherry and bourbon were gone. They talked about their families, the wedding, Dry Springs, and as good friends do, they talked about anything else that came to mind.

After finishing her third cup of coffee, Maria said, "I better head back and check on Cat and Enyeto. I still have some numbers to go over for your dad on how the store did last week."

Sophie smiled at Maria, knowing she liked working for her dad as much as he enjoyed having her there. "You know my dad never knew those numbers before you and Cisco came to work for him, so if you get them to him later in the morning, or never, he'll be just fine."

"I like doing them, especially for the last Monday of the month when it's time to order supplies from Denver. When your dad laughs and points out that he handled the ordering just fine before I started doing this, I point out the number of things stacked up in the storage room that he over-ordered and will take forever to sell, if they ever sell at all. Which reminds me, do you need me to order anything else for the wedding?"

Sophie couldn't imagine what else she might need for the wedding that Maria and the girls hadn't already thought of. She hugged Maria goodbye and watched her walk until she reached town and was out of sight. Realizing how cold she'd become, Sophie picked up the glasses, carried them into the house and locked the front door against the cold. Surprising herself, she left the unwashed glasses on the counter, took off her coat and shoes, and climbed into bed, keeping Brock's shirt on. She fell asleep holding the shirt tight around her body, willing Brock and Huck to be warm and safe—and to be home tomorrow.

Nine - Brock

A man riding the trails needs very few things, but the ones he does need are not optional—a good horse, a reliable pistol, an accurate rifle, a full canteen, plenty of food and a warm bedroll. As I wake this morning, the value of a good bedroll is in full evidence. Even with the protection of the overhang and warmth from the fire, it got very cold last night, well below freezing. The wind must have picked up too, because the heavy canvas wrap protecting me from the ground below and the elements above is covered with snow. The canvas, treated with wax, keeps out the rain and, in this case, the snow. And between the canvas, two heavy wool blankets and the full set of clothes I slept in, the cold never got past my face. But even though the wind has died down to nothing, the cold hasn't gone anywhere.

Wolf is gone, probably out hunting. I take a peek at Horse and see she's still close to the picketed horses and looking relaxed, which lets me know that, besides the three of us, there's no one close to our camp. Huck is being loudly scolded by an early morning magpie as he walks back into camp with full canteens, his Colt strapped to his side. I doubt after this week that he'll ever be caught out of town without his gun. He's shown he can handle it, but it still gnaws at me that a thirteen-year-old now needs to wear a gun. No doubt, this will be one of the many things that Sophie and I will be talking about when we get back to town.

I'm used to Cisco being up early, but I'm a little surprised Huck's up before me—for the first time on this trip. But it's good to see him moving around and doing his share of the work. Neither Cisco nor I would have said a word if he wasn't up to helping, but it's a good sign that he is. Huck and I still need to talk about what happened last night, but we'll be riding for a few hours this morning, so we should have plenty of time then.

The night, having already given way to predawn gray, is about to be completely replaced as the sun is rising over the mountains. My thoughts drift back to Frank, and I'm reminded to be grateful to see the sunrise. It is guaranteed to no man, in town or on the trail, but it's especially sweet to see on the trail, though it's sometimes easy to forget that, at least for me. I wonder if Frank noted the sunrise yesterday, or the sunset, no way of knowing he'd never see another one. I hate that Frank has seen his last, but I know now I'll do what I have to do to make that square. Some might say having killed the men who killed Frank paid that debt, but I figure it won't be right until the man who ordered the attack is taken care of. And after a night of thinking, and very little sleep, I'm convinced that man is Francisco Chavez.

Saying good morning to Huck and Cisco, who's already got the bacon and coffee going, I reach over and grab my boots, shaking them carefully to make sure no local critters moved in during the night. I slip off my moccasins and pull on my boots. As I'm packing my gear away, we all remain pretty quiet. We'll be back in Dry Springs this afternoon, back with our families, and we'll have to explain Frank's death. And for me, since we still don't know exactly what's happening, I have to figure out what to do next.

I walk down to the creek, picking up a frayed willow stick to use for a toothbrush, since I seem to have lost mine in all the confusion last night. The creek is quiet and smooth, and I can see my reflection as well as if I had a mirror. The man looking back at me needs a bath and a shave, but I don't have a razor, and as much as I enjoy taking a bath, that creek is far too cold for me to even think about jumping in. I splash some water on my face, brush my teeth and walk back to camp, where Cisco and Huck are finishing up their breakfast. I eat while they load up their gear, and we're back on the trail about the same time you'd say we went from dawn to day.

The conversation warms up with the sun, though we seem to be talking about anything other than what happened last night. Since last night was a first for both Cisco and Huck, I figure to let them deal with it in their own ways, though I know that if Huck doesn't bring it up, at some point I have to. Killing a man, for any reason, is hard on a good man, and Huck is a good man. I want to make sure he doesn't start thinking wrong about what happened and have that set inside him in a way it can't come out. But for now, I'll let him wait until he's ready, hoping that's the best thing to do.

We're making pretty good time, and our first stop isn't until close to noon. We water the horses and let them take a good roll, but everyone seems more interested in getting home quickly than in having lunch. We each grab a biscuit to chew on, and I'm not even able to finish my cigar before Huck is saddling the horses and we're back on the trail.

After a couple hours of easy riding, we're back on top of the little hill that overlooks Dry Springs. It's late enough in the afternoon that school is out, so Sophie will be home. I turn to say something to Huck, just in time to see him drop the lead line on the extra horses, put the spurs to Spirit and race off toward the house in a gallop.

Cisco looks at me, smiling. "I guess he's anxious to see his mom."

"I guess he is. You probably want to see Maria right away too. You ride straight away over to the general store."

I pick up the lead line Huck dropped. "And I'll take the horses to the livery."

Predictably, Cisco starts to tell me that he'll stay and help, but I smile and shake my head. He reaches out, shakes my hand, and then, as quick as Regalo can carry him, he rides off to find Maria.

I sit up on the hill for a couple of minutes, as much to try and gather my thoughts as to allow Huck a little extra time with Sophie. I ride down into town, stopping at the livery, just like I did the first time I ever saw Dry Springs. Looking back on that day, I don't know where I thought I'd be these few months later, but riding back into Dry Springs probably wouldn't have made the list. Tom sees me with all the horses and comes running out to help.

"Hello, Mr. Clemons. You got more horses than you left with."

"Hi, Tom. We do have some extras. I need you to take care of all of these horses. Give them a good rubdown, and they all get a bait of corn."

"OK. Where's Huck?"

"He's up at the house, with his mom. How about when you finish up here with the horses, you come up to the house and say hi? He could use a friend. If he doesn't feel much like talking, ask him about the bear."

I know Tom wants to ask me, but I glance back at the horses, just as Shawn is making his way out front, so Tom yells a quick "yessir" and is already moving the horses inside, no doubt his mind racing with questions about a bear.

"Welcome back, Brock. Looks like you've got some extra horses. Going into the horse trading business?"

"Thanks, Shawn. We're are going to be selling these four, so keep your ears open for anyone who may be looking."

"Of course. Curious how you came upon three unbranded, shoed horses." Smiling, he adds, "Must be a story behind that."

Up until right now, I'd been so focused on seeing Sophie, taking care of Huck, and trying to figure out what was happening and what I needed to do that I completely forgot I was going to have to explain to the town about what happened to Frank and, I guess, why we had these horses. I realize right away this is not a story I want to tell at all, much less over and over.

"Shawn, there is, but it's not a good story. Can you do me a favor?"

Shawn loses his smile, but not his curiosity. "Of course."

"Once you and Tom have finished up with the horses, let the men know I'd like to see them at the Dusty Rose in about an hour. Got some things we need to talk about."

"Sure, Brock. Do Cisco and Frank already know?"

"Cisco doesn't, so please ask him. He'll be over at the store with Maria." I hesitate for a moment, knowing this is going to be hard. "Shawn, Frank was killed last night—and it was no accident. Worse than that, I don't think it's over."

Shawn's face is immediately covered with questions.

"I know you want to know, but I've got to ride over and say hi to Sophie. Please don't say anything about Frank. I want to tell everyone at the same time and make sure no rumors get started. I'm going to need some help, but I don't know yet what it is."

Shawn chokes back his questions and, with a quick "See you in an hour," turns and heads back into the barn. I'm alone, for only the second time this week, and I take moment to gather my thoughts. As excited as I am about seeing Sophie, I dread having to tell her what happened and what Huck did. I think back to two days ago when all I had to worry about was how to tell her about Huck and the bear. Now I have to tell her, unless Huck already has, that because of me, we were ambushed, and Huck killed a man.

I ride up to the house and see Sophie on the porch with Huck, who I notice for the first time is taller than her, holding on tight. I can tell by the perfect smile on her face that Huck hasn't told her anything, but as she looks up at my face, I can tell by her reaction that she already knows there are things to tell.

Ten - Brock

Only yesterday, I was dreaming about this moment, seeing Sophie again after a week on the trail. And now, while I'm happy to see her and need to be with her, I'm dreading it. Huck lets go of his mom and turns to me.

"Huck, can you take care of Horse and Regalo? They've had a long ride. Extra bait of corn for each, please."

I hand Huck Horse's reins and switch places with him, holding onto Sophie, wondering if there's a way I can never let go. In the way that she does, without saying a word, she lets me know that we're gonna be OK, that we're gonna get through whatever it is that I haven't told her yet.

I tell her I love her and ask her for a glass of bourbon. She tells me she loves me too and turns to get the bourbon, and probably knowing all of her questions will be answered as soon as I can collect my thoughts, she asks none. I take my seat and spend the couple of minutes she's gone lighting up a cigar and gathering my thoughts. She's back as I finish lighting the cigar, but I'm nowhere near ready to have this conversation.

"Sophie, for reasons you'll understand in a few minutes, I've got to be down at the Rose in less than an hour, so as hard as this is, I'm just going to tell you what happened and what I'm afraid might be happening. When I get back, we can talk all night."

She returns with my bourbon, none for herself, takes a seat and my hand.

"Last night, as we were setting up camp, we were attacked by four men, and Frank was killed. We killed all four, buried Frank and rode on for a while before making another camp."

She catches her breath and tightens her grip on my hand, but she doesn't say a word, her eyes glancing quickly to the barn and Huck—as if to ensure he's still OK—and then back to me.

"Is Cisco OK?"

"Yes, he's with Maria now. Sophie, there's more—and it's not good."

From the very first day I met Sophie, I knew she was stronger than me. No matter what needed to be said, no matter how hard, or how painful, she expected—demanded—to be told straight whatever it was she needed to hear. And she wasted no time, or words, if she was the one that had to do the telling. So, I kill the glass of bourbon, take a long draw on my cigar, look the woman I love in the eye and tell her.

"The four men? They were from Chavez's ranch. Cisco recognized the foreman, Miguel, who died last. At the end, as he was dying, he told us that Chavez was gunning for me and wasn't going to stop. And Sophie, the worst part? Miguel? Huck's the one who killed him."

I know she has dozens of questions and wants to ask all of them at once, but she doesn't. She stands up, reaches over, kisses me hard and tells me, "You go down to the Rose, and do what you need to do to take care of this. The men will be with you. I have to take care of Huck."

And with that, she turns and walks toward the barn, seeming to be willing herself not to run. Huck looks up, and I can tell he knows immediately that I've told her. He closes the corral gate and, looking more like the boy he should be than the man he has been forced to become, once again grabs onto his mom, holding on like he may never let go. Knowing he needs her more than he needs me right now, I step into the kitchen, make a quick sandwich and start walking to town. Looking back, I see that Huck and Sophie haven't moved.

Wanting to be with them, but knowing I can't, I force myself to look away, to turn my attention to the Dusty Rose and try to figure out what needs to happen. The last time we had a meeting like this, the town was under attack, and I was new and trying to save it. Now, it's me who's under attack, for reasons I still don't understand, and my problems, sadly, are now also the town's problems.

I walk into the Dusty Rose, still unsure of what I'm going to say, or even what I hope will happen. I say a few hellos, shake a few hands and work my way to the bar. Without asking, Will pours me a bourbon, which I gratefully accept. I reflect for a moment on our home, Ray's store, Hattie's and even Thurm's bank, but somehow, when it comes down to it, the Dusty Rose is the bedrock of Dry Springs. It was the headquarters for the battle against Kurt, from the planning to the actual battle. It's served as the town church for months. And once again, when we need to meet, this is where we wind up.

In a way, this reminds me of when we met here to talk about Kurt and his gang, but it's also very different. While the men don't know yet why I've called them here, they know it's important, and I know it's a different group of men than those who cowered before Kurt. About half of the men are those who were here before, and half are newer. There's only one who I can't remember ever seeing before, and while he seems familiar in some way, there's no time to stop and talk. Most of the ranchers and farmers aren't here, as we couldn't get word to them in time, but they'll find out soon enough.

"Men, I'm sorry to have to call you all together on such short notice, but it's important. Cisco, Huck and I just rode into town, and as most of you probably already know, Frank wasn't with us. He was killed last night, murdered by four men who attacked our camp. We killed all four of them, and Cisco recognized one as the foreman down at the ranch he used to work at. Even worse, his last words seemed to mean that they were gunning for me and that they're not done. Since they were willing to kill all of us last night, I'm afraid if they come for me again, some of you might be in danger. I don't know why they're after me, but I aim to find out, and I aim to take care of this. I'm not asking any of you for anything, at least not right now, but I felt you needed to know."

I'm looking out at the men, listening to the murmurs and waiting for the questions that have to come, when Will taps me from behind on the shoulder. The men quiet down.

"You say there were four of them?"

"Yep."

"Were they all Mex?"

"Yep."

"Brock, there were four riders in town a few days ago. They hung around the bar, stayed at Portis' place and kept pretty much to themselves. They did ask a little about you, but I figured they were more of those who read about you in the papers and were curious about what happened with Kurt. I never thought…"

"There's no way you could have known. No reason to think there was anything more than you thought."

I turn back to the men, just in time to see the batwing doors open and, framed against the setting sun, Huck standing there. He takes a moment, let's his eyes adjust, and without a word, walks up to the bar and stands next to me and Cisco.

Ken James, Tom's dad, looks around the room, then at me. He asks a question that is fair to ask and I know is on others' minds as well.

"Brock, we all love Huck, but is this a place for a boy to be?"

Before I can answer, the front doors are pushed open again. Looking into the setting sun, I see the woman I love standing in the doorway. She must have followed Huck down and heard Ken's question. She looks around the bar and then directly at Ken. In a strong, feminine voice, with no hint of anger but leaving no room for discussion, she says, "Ken, you're right—it's no place for a boy. But Huck stays."

Sophie looks at me and then at Huck, takes one last look around the bar to see if anyone has anything to say, simply says, "Thank you," and lets herself back out the door. There's a little buzz, but not really much of one, and the three of us stay where we are, at the bar.

Big Irish McClaskey stands up, reminding me why he's called Big Irish. His voice fills the bar. "This time, we're with you from the first day." He pauses, looks around and gives anyone who dares an opportunity to share a different opinion. No one does.

Big Irish continues. "What can we do?" As I prepare to answer, I notice the one man I don't know at all quietly letting himself out, but with the sun now set, I have no idea where he's going or why he left. Something about him nags at me, but I need to focus here.

"Thanks, Big. I'm sorry it's come to this and even sorrier I don't know what 'it' is. I came down here to warn you, not to ask for help, but it's good to know you're here if we need it." I look at Cisco on my right and Huck on my left, making it clear who "we" is, as much for each of them as for everyone else who's here.

"The one thing I do ask for now is to keep your eyes out. If you see anyone new in town, like Will saw those four men, let me or Cisco know right away. If Chavez really is behind this, he has plenty of men, and whatever it is that drove him to this is only going to get worse when he finds out we killed his men.

"Those of you who live outside of town, if you see any strange riders, let me know right away. I'll be making a couple of circles every day around the outskirts of town, looking to cut any new sign."

Will steps out from behind the three of us and announces, "I'll ride with you every morning, 'cept Sundays. You can use an extra set of eyes, and I could use to spend some more time on a horse."

Cisco starts to say he'll ride with me too, but I cut him off. "Cisco, you need to stay in town. You're the only one who will recognize the men if Chavez sends anybody new into town." I pause. "Unless it's Diego. I'll know him."

Reverend Matt jumps in. "I'll ride with you in the afternoon. We're busy with the church but getting close to being done, and like Will, I could use some more time in a saddle. I'm thinking maybe you should deputize Will, Cisco and me so if anything happens out there, it's all legal, and if you or Clybs needs help in town, same thing."

The idea makes sense to me, so I tell them to meet me at the sheriff's office after the meeting.

"Boys, thank you. Hopefully, nothing comes of this, but if it does, I'd be lying if I didn't say it feels good having you with me. Now, two more things—one good, one not—and then how about a round on me before we head home?"

As it is any time, in any bar, for almost any reason, the suggestion of someone buying a round is met with great enthusiasm. It has been my experience that for many beer drinkers it's a rare occasion when they might try a top-shelf whiskey, but it would be good for them and good for Will. I've always thought that if you're not willing to pay for more than beer, you shouldn't offer to buy a round. I feel great just thinking about how far we've come as a town in the past few months and, oddly enough, how something like this, every once in a while, is a great way to keep people working together.

"We buried Frank where he was shot, did the best we could with the grave. So that all of you know, we're selling the three horses from the killers, along with Frank's, and sending the money to his family in Guatemala. Thurm, I'm gonna need to talk to you about where Frank lived, find out if it was his or not. Wanna send as much as we can to his family. We read a letter from his brother, and they're hungry. Figure we can help. If any of you want to buy the horses, any of Frank's gear or any of the weapons from the killers, talk to Shawn. Whatever price he sets is what we're going with."

Huck looks up at me.

"I'd like to buy Frank's saddle."

Lowering my voice just a little, I say, "Huck, you have a saddle."

"Frank told me on this trip that his saddle was his favorite possession. He told me it's an 1859 McClellan and it fit him perfectly. Said he rode it when he was in the war. Even if it doesn't fit me yet, I'd like to have it." He pauses, looking at Cisco and then back at me. "Please."

Beginning to understand what this means to Huck, I look away from him and toward the men. "If no one objects, Huck would like to buy Frank's saddle." No one says anything, so I turn to Shawn.

"Figure out a fair price and let me know how much."

Huck jumps in. "Shawn, please let me know how much the saddle is. I'll be paying for it." Shawn quickly glances at me, and when I don't object, he looks back at Huck and says, "I'll set it aside for you."

"OK, for everything else, let's wait until morning. Just stop by and see Shawn. Know that every dollar goes to Frank's family. Matt, if you could please come up and say a few words for Frank."

Matt steps to the front and we all bow our heads. I know he's been working hard on his first sermon in the new church, but the words he said up here with no time to prepare came fast and rang true, and everyone agreed it was a great way to say goodbye to Frank.

"For the good news, let me remind everyone that a week from Sunday, Cisco and I are getting hitched."

The room breaks up into laughter, and I realize that we all needed a relief from the tension and that with my statement I'd given them the outlet.

"Now boys," I say as I put my arm around Cisco. "You all know we'll be bringing Maria and Sophie with us. Just plan on coming out in the morning for the Rev's sermon, and we'll go right from that to the weddings. We'll be feeding you from sunup to last home, so plan on staying all day."

And with that, my bar tab started.

Scott Harris

Eleven - Brock

I left the house before Sophie woke up, and I'm not even sure I didn't leave before I was really awake. This morning, like most of last night, is a painful blur.

Will and I ride out of town, our heads pounding. While I bought the first round last night, it definitely was not the last one. I sent Huck walking home when Nolan picked up the second round, and then Thurm surprised everyone by buying the third. The surprise wasn't from the generosity— Thurm is often generous with the people of Dry Springs. But up until recently, he wouldn't even go into the Rose unless it was for a town meeting. I still haven't grown used to seeing him occasionally sitting in the Rose, usually nursing a single beer for an hour or two, and still never playing cards, but there nonetheless—and now he's buying a round.

I remember Will buying a round for the house after Thurm, and then I really don't remember much after that. It's been a while since I got good and drunk, and this feeling of wanting to crawl off of Horse, curl up in a ball and sleep for two days on the side of the trail reminds me of why. But, maybe, in some way, I needed it. Either way, Will's feeling it too, and so while we both try to shake the cobwebs out of our heads, the only sound is our horses and the painfully loud birds.

I have this almost gagging feeling in my mouth, like I'm chewing on a combination of cotton and sand, combined with what I believe is a very real fear that my head might explode. But my biggest regret is that I was in no condition to have the conversation last night with Sophie about everything that happened on the trip and what my plans are for ending whatever this is with Chavez. She is a patient woman, but it will certainly still be in my best interests to not test the limits of that patience any further than I already have. So, I plan to be home this afternoon when she gets back from school, ready to talk—and listen—until she's good and done.

Thinking about it now, I guess I had hoped when I traded the trail for Dry Springs that I had left behind that kind of sudden, cruel violence. Frank's death was a terrible reminder that that's not true, and it's my responsibility to see that it stops with Frank, that it's not brought any closer to my town, to my family. The meeting last night, at least before the rounds started, was a good idea, and so is the idea of doing these twice-a-day scouting trips around town. But it's not enough.

Will and I finish up the ride, discovering nothing new or out of the ordinary, and with almost no conversation. It's good to have a friend you can ride in comfortable silence with, although in fairness, it may have just been that we were both hurting too much to want to talk at all. Will rides straight to the Rose so he can get ready to open for the day, and I head to the livery. It's still early, so Shawn and Huck aren't in yet. I take these last quiet moments to rub Horse down, pick her hooves and even give her a peppermint candy, which she was introduced to by Huck and has come to love and, after a ride, to expect.

I finish up with Horse and walk over to Ray's store. His reaction to my mistakenly letting the door slam reminds me that Will and I are not the only two men suffering a bit this morning. A mumbled "morning" and a nod in return seem to be about all either of us can muster for now. I pick up a couple of things we need for the house and walk back up, leaving Horse to spend some time in the corral with the other horses. By the time I get there, Sophie has left for school, and somehow, I missed Huck too.

I put the supplies away and take a long look at my bed, which is certainly calling to me. As much as I want to take a good, long nap, that wouldn't be, unfortunately, sending the message to the town that I have this situation, whatever it is, covered. So, with one last glance at my very comfortable bed, I turn and head back to town. It's warmed up since Will and I got back, so I leave my coat at the house.

The first person I see is Cisco, who's on his way, slowly, to work at the store.

I ask, quietly, "How you feeling?"

"I have had better mornings, my friend."

This could refer to many different things, but as I look at Cisco's nearly closed eyes, I can tell at least part of it has to do with how much he had to drink last night. Remembering that I did not get around to doing the deputizing last night, I say, "Before you start work, let's go find Matt and Will and get you all deputized."

Cisco nods and steps quickly into the store, and I hear him tell Ray he'll be back in a few minutes and explain why. We walk next door to where the church is almost done and, not surprisingly, find Matt working away. Matt quickly joins us, and we turn back and head to the Dusty Rose. Will seems happy to take a break from swamping out the Rose, and we all head over to the sheriff's office. It still feels a bit odd to be a sheriff, and I'm also not used to having an office and a jail. We have two brand-new cells, built to hold the territory's worst outlaws, but as of yet, I haven't even locked anyone up for a good old-fashioned bar fight.

Clybs is already in, but he's at least half asleep, and the other half doesn't look ready for much of anything. Seems like we're all paying the price for last night. I don't actually have any deputy badges, having used the only one we had on Clybs, so I'll need to order some more from Denver. The ceremony doesn't take long.

"I'm asking all of you to become deputies. You pretty much know what's involved, and you especially know what we're dealing with now. Do you accept?"

Quick yeses from everyone, and Dry Springs has three new deputies, all good men. As Clybs is shaking everyone's hand, I remember how important it was for him to become my deputy. Not wanting this to take away from that in any way, I add one more thing.

"Clybs, now that we've got three new deputies, someone's got to train them and watch over them. I'm too busy to handle that, so it's going to fall on you. I'm also making you senior deputy, and the town will be giving you a five dollar a month raise"

Clybs seems to stand just a little bit taller, smiles and shakes my hand.

I look at the other three. "You're all working for free." With smiles all around, the kind easily shared among friends, the four of us head out, leaving Clybs in charge and me hoping he'll stay awake. Will heads back to the Rose, Matt to the church and Cisco to the store. I walk across the street to the bank.

"Good morning, Cat. Is Thurm in?"

"Sure, Brock. I'll tell him you're here. You feeling OK?"

Sadly, the question confirms that I look just about how I feel.

Cat has been doing some work for Thurm, mostly in the mornings. The town is growing and so is the bank, and Thurm thought it would be nice to have a teller working every morning. It's just another sign of Dry Springs' growth, and it doesn't appear it's going to be slowing down for a while. It seems that each time someone new moves into Dry Springs, or close enough to town that this is where they shop and do business, they know of others, mostly from around Denver, who are thinking of making the same move. Thurm says he loves the growth and that the town is starting to approach a size that matches the large bank he originally built. He says he thinks we'll have well over a thousand people by the end of next year, and maybe even get close this year, which seems a little hard to imagine—but Thurm works hard to make sure he's right about these things, so maybe he'll be right here too.

I'm not sure how I feel about that. I came here from London looking for my dad and spent a little time in New York and St. Louis. And while I didn't find my dad, I did find wide-open territory and open trails, and I learned I prefer that to a city. Dry Springs isn't what you'd call a city yet, but the way it's going, it's going to be a pretty good-sized town, pretty soon.

Thurm walks out from his office, maybe looking the worst of all of us.

"Good morning, Brock. I don't know how you men drink on a regular basis. It's expensive, and I fear it will be days before I am myself again." He leans back against the counter, which now seems to be the only thing holding him up.

I smile for the first time today, remembering that others have it worse than I do.

"Thurm, I'm sorry you're feeling poorly. I know it doesn't seem like it, but you'll wake up tomorrow feeling great. I don't want to lie to you though—you'll be hurting all day today."

Thurm's look borders on desperation, and I suspect I may be looking at his first—and last—morning after. While I feel for him, I have to get back to work, and first I need a little information.

"Thurm, when we've sold everything, will you be able to send the money down to Frank's family in Guatemala?"

"Yes, as long as you know their names and the city."

"I do, thank you. And what is the status of Frank's property?"

"He owes the bank about one hundred dollars, but then it's free and clear. I thought maybe you'd take one hundred dollars from the sale money and pay off the land?"

"Seems fair to me. We'll just have to figure out what to do with the property. You have any ideas?"

"Brock, my only idea today is to stay out of the sun, away from all noise—have you ever noticed how noisy this town is in the morning?!—and somehow survive until we close up the bank and I can go home, collapse on the bed and decide if I'm ever going to step foot in Will's place—or even speak to him—again."

"OK, Thurm, I'm feeling pretty much the same way. Only difference is, I've already accepted that we'll both be back there, sooner than later, and if my past is any indicator of the future, it's not the last time I'll have a morning like this. I'll come by again tomorrow, and maybe we'll both be feeling better."

With that, I head down to the store, hoping to have one of those new Black Rose cigars from the Pamperin Cigar Co. out of La Crosse, Wisconsin, that Ray has been carrying lately. At four bits, they're expensive, and even though they're worth it, I still can't afford them every day. Sometimes Ray takes a little pity on me and my small sheriff's salary and throws in a couple of extra for free. This isn't one of those days, so I toss Ray a Liberty Dollar and take two cigars, one for right now and one for tonight. Ray, using the owner's prerogative, helps himself to one and follows me out to the porch. We each take our regular chair, which gives us both a great view of most of the street. I've got to be watching anyway, so I might as well do it with Ray and a cigar.

We both take our time lighting up our cigars, as men sometimes do when they have, or need, some time to think. Today, it's both. Just as I'm finishing up, Ray takes a nice, long draw on his Black Rose, keeps looking across the street at nothing and asks, "What happened on this trip?"

I set my feet up on the railing. Since it's just past noon, the sun has worked its way far enough west to be over the store and under the porch, and it feels good after the cold of the last few days on the trail. I take my time telling Ray about the entire trip, including Huck and the bear and as much as I know about everything that happened with the Chavez men. Ray confirms what I already suspected about his daughter, that I'm not going to have fun telling her about what happened—and almost happened—with Huck. He asks if I talked to Huck about the man he killed, and I tell him that so far Huck hasn't wanted to talk about, so I've left him alone.

"Brock, I'm guessing Huck hasn't said anything because he doesn't know what to say. He's a special kid. Heck, he's more of a man at thirteen than many of us are that have had that title for quite a few more years. But, he's still thirteen and he needs you to walk him through this. Not me, not Sophie—you. He knows you've been through this. He looks up to you, and you were there. Plus, you're his dad now. Anyway, you can't let this fester like a wound. If it sticks too long, the poison will take and he'll never get past this."

Both of our cigars have gone out, so I think about what Ray said as we relight them. He's right of course, and I guess I knew that before he said anything. That means I have two tough conversations coming up this afternoon. We sit quietly and finish up our cigars.

"Thanks, Ray. I'll see you tonight at the house."

I leave him on the porch and walk next door to the church. Matt is hard at work, wrapping up the final details, but the place already looks beautiful. "Matt, will you be ready to go in about an hour? I want to be back before Sophie and Huck get out of school."

"Just give me ten minutes notice, and I'll be ready to go. Hope nothing happens. Not sure how steady my gun hand would be today."

"Mine either Rev, mine either. My guess is that Chavez doesn't even know yet that his men have been killed. I think we've got a few days before we really have to worry. Might as well get used to checking every day though."

I walk to the other end of town, stopping on the way to check on Clybs, who's still struggling to see and think clearly, and then I head over to Hattie's. Even though I didn't have breakfast, I'm still not hungry. But I've got a little time before Matt and I head out, and I've heard people say that a piece of one of Nerissa's apple pies can cure 'bout any sickness, including what ails me. I've got nothing to lose, so I take a table tucked away in the corner and ask Nerissa for a cup of coffee, extra hot, and piece of pie, large.

Twelve - Dusty

Dusty Stevens had heard enough and quietly left the Dusty Rose, knowing now what he needed to do. He walked down to the livery—which, since everyone was at the town meeting, was empty—left a dollar on the counter to more than square up his account, saddled up his chestnut mustang, Smokey, and headed toward Coyote Creek, the fastest way to Santa Fe.

Dusty knew he was dying.

He had tuberculosis, which up until a couple of years before had commonly been called consumption. No matter what you called it, you couldn't beat it, and Dusty, having seen many a man—and some women—die from the same disease, knew he had, at best, only a few months to live. He had always been physically strong and able to lift more than most men, won far more fights than he lost, and survived things in the territory that most men couldn't imagine living through. But now his once powerful body was betraying him. He was losing weight quickly and was frequently racked with debilitating coughs, which now occasionally included spots of blood, and he could feel his strength draining from his deteriorating body. The ride to Santa Fe was going to be hard, but he knew he had to do it.

It had been more than twenty years since Dusty had abandoned Brock and his mother.

He loved her and he loved Brock, but after two years of living in London, he came to realize, and then accept, that he loved the West more. The territory called to him more than fatherhood, even more than Isabella, the only woman he ever loved. And so, in the most cowardly act of his life, he left his son in the care of his wife, and his wife in the care of her brother, Jacob. He knew they would be fine, and he even left with Isabella's blessing, but that was no excuse for what he did. Over the years, he'd been tempted a number of times to return to London, once even making it as far as New York before turning back— but he had promised Isabella when he left that he wouldn't return, since she feared the complication it would almost certainly bring to Brock's life. He often wondered if he used the promise as an excuse to not return, especially since he already had been willing to break his first promise to her by leaving her and Brock.

It was almost two years ago when Dusty first became aware that his son had come over from London and was looking for him. The West was a massive area of land, but a small community. There were very few secrets in the towns of the West and even very few secrets between towns, so when Brock arrived in St. Louis, ironically where Dusty had first met Isabella, and started asking questions about him, it didn't take long for Dusty to hear about it.

Embarrassed by his actions of twenty years ago, he avoided Brock at every turn. He did linger long enough in Denver to play in a poker game at a table next to Brock, more focused on watching his son than on his game—which cost him plenty of money, but did let him see how his son had grown. He even considered introducing himself, but by then the tuberculosis had taken over his body and he just couldn't bring himself to meet Brock in that condition, so once again, he rode away.

But finally, knowing he'd seen his last Christmas and was coming to the end of the trail, Dusty decided it was time to meet his son. He'd read about him in the papers after the gun battle with Kurt and his men, so he knew where to find him. And after one last high-stakes poker game in Santa Fe and one final trip to the orphanage in Tucson, he made his way to Dry Springs. Brock wasn't in town when Dusty arrived, but he quickly learned, in the way that happens in a small town, that Brock was the sheriff, was engaged to a woman named Sophie and had adopted a son, Huck. He planned to introduce himself to Brock. He also hoped to meet Sophie and Huck and, if things went well, maybe even be invited to the wedding he knew was coming up. It was a lot to hope for, but hope was all he had left.

But all of that changed in the Dusty Rose when he heard Brock tell the story of what happened to him on the trail and that Chavez was involved, which meant that somehow, though Dusty didn't know exactly how, he was involved too.

And so, after an uneventful few days, but a very hard ride, Dusty rode into Santa Fe, stopping first at the livery.

"Skip, good to see you. Can you take care of Smokey for me?"

"Sure, Dusty. How long?"

"Just for the night. Leaving at first light. You'll be here?"

Skip just looked up at Dusty and smiled. It seemed that Skip was always there, and it had become a bit of a running joke between him and Dusty. Dusty, only half kiddingly, had often wondered if Skip had a twin brother. It just didn't seem possible that one man could work that many hours. No matter what time you stopped by, Skip was either working on a horse or playing his dinged-up harmonica, and either way, Dusty had never ridden in and not found him there.

"Make sure he gets a good rubdown and some extra corn. Long day coming up tomorrow."

Skip, surprised, was a little insulted that Dusty felt he had to tell him about the rubdown or the corn. "Sure, Dusty. See you with the sun."

Trusting Skip with his gear, Dusty took a clean shirt and his toothbrush and walked slowly to the hotel. Dusty was known at the De Vargas, so as soon as he walked in, the clerk arranged for him to have his regular room, which, unknown to Dusty, was the same room Brock had stayed in when he visited Santa Fe last year.

It was early afternoon, and the men Dusty wanted to talk to wouldn't be at the Red Garter until later in the evening. So Dusty set his toothbrush on the counter, stripped down to his long johns, hung his clothes over the chair and settled in for a long nap, trusting that he'd wake up in time for his evening meal before he walked over to the Red Garter.

And in the way sunrise wakes so many, sunset woke Dusty. For the last couple of years, since he first got sick and could no longer do the ranch work, or trapping, he had loved for so long, his new job had started when the sun went down. He'd trained himself to sleep during the day and wake in the evening, which is when the best poker and faro games got started.

Dusty got dressed, went downstairs and had a small dinner, though it seemed that these past few weeks he ate more out of habit than enjoyment, or even hunger. Because it irritated his cough so much, he'd given up his lifetime habit of smoking a cigar after almost every evening meal, and he passed on having a drink because the taste was no longer worth the price he'd pay later. More than once, Dusty thought it would have been better to have been not quite so fast with a gun and have died a little sooner. The prospect of rotting away in a bed, alone, scared Dusty far more than any gunman or band of Indians he had ever faced. In recent months, he'd often wondered which small town he would be in when he finally woke up one morning, finally unable to drag himself out of bed one last time, using his last few dollars to purchase the care of strangers as his life slowly ebbed.

Shaking those thoughts from his mind once again, Dusty worked his way over to the Red Garter and took a seat at what had become his regular table on his frequent visits to Santa Fe. The game was moving slowly, as they often did early in the evening, and Dusty eased himself into a chair and the game. He knew most of the regulars, and since it was a Saturday night, they were all there, with one notable exception. Dusty thought the men were looking at him a bit differently than they had in the past, but the game continued and he joined easily into the conversation.

Jeremy Binns was as friendly as always and said business had never been better at his general stores. Ron Gordon, who ran the *Santa Fe New Mexican* newspaper, said the same thing, that Santa Fe was continuing to grow and all of the businesses, including the paper, were benefitting. Dusty met Devin Darnell for the first time, though he had seen him in the Red Garter before, just not at this table. Darnell had fought with General Henry Sibley for the few days back in '62 when the Confederates had held Santa Fe. They'd been defeated and driven from Santa Fe in the Battle of Glorieta Pass, where Darnell earned his lifelong limp from what he always maintained was a lucky Union shot. He stayed in Santa Fe long past his recovery, building a life and a small, but profitable, blacksmith and woodworking shop.

Dan Pulos, who owns one of the larger cattle ranches in the area, bordered on one side by Chavez's, was strangely quiet, and just as Dusty was trying to figure out why, Sheriff Geoff Dean walked into the Red Garter and, seeing Dusty, walked over to him immediately.

"Evening, Dusty. Wasn't sure we'd see you here again."

"Always happy to see you, Sheriff, and I'm not sure I've ever been to town and not seen you."

Dean didn't match Dusty's smile. "You might not be so happy tonight. Mind joining me over in the corner for a drink and a chat?"

Dusty, trusting the men he played with, took only enough chips to buy a couple of drinks and left the rest to hold his spot. He followed Dean to a quiet corner and a table he'd never seen anyone sit at if they weren't with the sheriff.

The sheriff ordered a couple of bourbons, and Dusty didn't stop him. Mostly out of habit, he even pulled a cigar out of his shirt pocket, though he didn't light it. He sat quietly, waiting, knowing the sheriff had something on his mind.

"Dusty, what is there between you and Chavez?"

"Other than cards, nothing. We've played quite a few games in the past year or two."

"And you won every time, usually big?"

"Every time except the first—took me that night to figure out how he was cheating."

Dean stopped and looked at Dusty. "He was cheating?"

"Yessir."

"Why didn't you say anything?"

"Sheriff, since I took sick, I've had to make my living playing cards. One of the things I've learned is that it's easier to beat a cheat if he doesn't know you know he's cheating. I've just learned to figure out who and how and then quietly use that to my advantage. Chavez was OK at it, though he wouldn't have lived through a big game in Denver or San Francisco. Here, it was our little secret. Unfortunately for him, he thought it was just his little secret."

"You took him for a lot of money."

"Yessir I did. He still owes me some from the last game. Part of the reason I'm here."

"Well, sorry to say, you won't be collecting that money, but that's not the biggest problem you have with Chavez."

Dusty sat still and watched the sheriff, using the patience he learned at the poker tables, knowing there was more to come.

"Dusty, Chavez lost everything, including his ranch. He left a few days ago, taking some cattle, all of his gunmen and a few of his cowboys. He left behind the ranch, the people who lived and worked there, and a mountain of debt. I'm guessing he didn't know as much about cattle or cards as he thought he did."

Dusty started thinking about what he'd heard at the Dusty Rose, but again, with a gamblers patience, decided to hear what the sheriff had to say before offering any information.

"I'm sorry to hear that sheriff, but I don't see what that means to me, other than I won't be collecting what he owes me." And with a little smile, he added, "And I won't be winning as much in the future."

"Dusty, when he left, there was a rumor he sent four men to Tucson to kill you. Everyone, including Chavez, knows you head to Tucson after a big win, though no one knows why. I sent a wire to the sheriff there, to get you word. He couldn't find you, but he knew you and had heard that there were men in town asking about you. Since you're sitting here, it's obvious they didn't find you."

"Sheriff, we both know I'm dying, but I'm not dead yet, so don't be so sure that if they had found me it would've been them who'd ridden back. Now, I know I took some money off of Chavez, but not enough to cause him to lose his ranch. Why's he gunning for me?"

"Dusty, I don't know for sure—none of us do—but a couple of the boys at your regular game said he seemed to be losing his mind a little, and part of that was somehow blaming you for everything. Fair or not, he did send some men looking for you."

"We'll, they didn't find me, and I'll be gone in the morning. But, Sheriff, I make my living reading people now, and I'd go all in betting you have something more to tell me."

"I do, so I'll just get to it. Dusty, the worst-kept secret at the Red Garter is that Brock Clemons is your son, that he's been looking for you and that you didn't want to be found. The boys all like you, and we figured it's none of our business, so no one said anything, to you or him. But Chavez knew too, and I guess him and your boy had a little dustup a while back, and Chavez's gun hand, Diego, was in it too. When he left here, one of the cowboys who stayed behind told Dan Pulos that Chavez was heading up to Dry Springs to start over, and the first thing he was going to do was kill your boy—unless it was already done. I just found that out today, and I figured maybe he sent some gun hands that way, same as he did to Tucson, but there's no telegraph in Dry Springs, so I had no way to warn him."

Dusty sat quiet for a moment, absorbing what Sheriff Dean had told him, confirming his worst fears. The same son he had abandoned more than twenty years ago and avoided for the past two years was now in danger because of him. Even worse, it appeared his new family was also not safe.

"Sheriff, Chavez did send some men, four of them. They ambushed my son and his son, a boy named Huck, as well as two of his friends, killing one. Chavez's men all died for their trouble. Do you know when Chavez left here and how many men he had with him?"

"He had himself, Diego, and I think two other gun hands, plus about a half dozen cowboys, pushing the cows he stole from Dan."

"Stole?

"Yes. Dan bought the ranch and all of the cattle for about fifty cents on the dollar. It wasn't enough to pay off all of Chavez's debt, but all of the big boys—Binns, the bank, and others—agreed to take what they could get and move on. Even then, Chavez snuck out about three days ago with maybe a hundred head that weren't his. I went to Dan to see what he wanted me to do, and he said to let it go, that it wasn't worth any men dying to get a few cattle back from a desperate man."

Dusty thanked the sheriff for the information, gathered his chips and said goodbye to the men from the game, and walked back to the hotel to get a good night's sleep before what he knew would be a tough ride back to Dry Springs.

Dawn found Dusty at the livery, where Skip already had Smokey saddled and ready to go. There was also a note for Dusty that the sheriff had left with Skip. It was a telegram from the Tucson sheriff.

The four men you asked about are dead.
Braced the wrong men.
Not as fast as they thought they were.

Thirteen - Brock

Nerissa's pie, in addition to tasting great, does seem to have some medicinal value, and I'm starting to feel a bit better. The ride with Matt is much more enjoyable than the one earlier today with Will, or at least not as miserable. Even the birds seem to have quieted down to a tolerable level. Matt, showing an understanding of human nature, or at least of me, seems kindly determined to talk about anything other than what happened with Chavez's men. And knowing I've got a long, and probably unpleasant, conversation coming up this afternoon with Sophie, I welcome the break.

The wedding is getting close, and Matt assures me the church will be ready. He's excited about every little detail of the church and clearly loves his job, which does seem like more of a calling for him, than it does a job. It's beginning to nag at me that I don't feel the same way about being sheriff. It's an honor to be the sheriff of Dry Springs, and I'm grateful to the town for the opportunity. But—and I'm not sure why, or even what it means for the future—I don't think I'm cut out to be a sheriff for the rest of my life.

Matt and I work our way back to the livery. I say my goodbyes as Matt turns his horse over to Shawn, and I ride Horse up to the house. Huck and Sophie aren't back from school quite yet, so I take my time brushing Horse before turning her loose in the corral to roll and stretch. I'm leaning on the fence poles, collecting my thoughts, enjoying the sun and the quiet, when I see Sophie making her way up the hill.

I start walking toward Sophie, and it strikes me that for the first time since I met her, I'm not excited about seeing her. It's certainly not her fault—she's done nothing wrong. And I don't think what happened on the trail was my fault, but I'm still not looking forward to having the conversation, especially having made her wait until today, which was my fault. As I get close, I look at her and simply say, "I'm sorry."

She responds with a small smile and takes my hand, and we walk the rest of the way to the house in silence, not an uncomfortable silence, but maybe both of us taking a couple of quiet minutes before we start.

I hang my gun belt on the peg by the door while Sophie gets the coffee boiling. It doesn't take long before the coffee's ready, and we decide to sit inside, each taking one of the comfortable leather chairs. I immediately want to close my eyes and take the nap that's been calling to me all day, but with my survival instinct, I sense that might not be the very best idea I've ever had. So, I sit up straight, take a sip of coffee and ask Sophie how her day was.

"Long."

"Is everything OK at school?"

"Yes. What happened with Huck?"

I am reminded, again, that Sophie isn't much for small talk when there are big things to talk about, so even though I might have preferred easing into this, I start right in and tell her everything that happened from the moment we rode into camp two nights ago until we got back to town yesterday. Then I tell her what decisions were made last night at the Dusty Rose, and last, I tell her about today— deputizing Matt, Cisco and Will, my conversation with Thurm, and my uneventful rides with Will and Matt.

Having not said a word as I told her everything that happened, she now asks, "Are you OK?"

"I'm worried about Huck and I'm paying the price for staying at the Dusty Rose too long last night, but yes, I'm OK."

"Good." I'm not sure if she means "Good, I'm glad you're OK," or "Good, I'm glad you're paying the price for last night." But, before I can ask her, or figure it out on my own, she keeps moving.

"What did Huck say when you talked to him about this?"

I noticed right away, the question wasn't, "Have you talked to Huck?" Instead, what Sophie was actually saying was, "Of course you spoke to Huck about something so important and something that will have such a huge impact on him. So, how did that conversation go?" I am instantly reminded of two things: how similar Sophie and Ray are and that I still have much to learn about being a father.

"I'll talk to him about this when he gets home from school."

I think I would prefer, much prefer, that Sophie was angry with me, rather than being disappointed in me. And while this isn't the time to ask, I'm guessing that right now she's certainly one of the two, and probably both.

Far too quietly, she asks, or states, "Our son was ambushed by murderers, watched a friend get shot and killed right in front of him, then shot and killed a man and probably a horse—all of this two days ago—and you plan to first talk to him this afternoon?"

Her question leaves no room for what she's going to consider a reasonable answer, and as I struggle to come with any answer, I am saved, at least temporarily, when we hear Huck and Tom climb the steps and take seats on the porch. The windows are open to allow the warmth of the first sunny day in a while into the house, so we can easily hear what the boys are saying. They are obviously continuing a conversation that probably started this morning when they first saw each other at the livery. Sophie reaches across and takes my hand, in a way that lets me know she loves me and that we're not done with this discussion, but also to be quiet so we can hear what the boys are saying.

"Brock killed one of them with a knife?!" The excitement is clear in Tom's voice.

"Yep. Remember his knife I showed you?" I look at Sophie, a bit surprised that Huck had gone through my stuff and showed my knife to Tom. It's a big knife—the blade is almost a foot long—so I can understand why he'd be curious, but I'm still surprised. We can't see the boys, but Tom must have nodded yes, because Huck continues.

"When Brock and Cisco were done, I went to get the horses, and I walked by him. You could see his throat in the moonlight. He was covered in blood, and so was the snow. There was steam coming off of him.

"I came back with the horses, and we moved to another camp. We didn't even bury them, just left them where they died. We did bury Frank, best we could. I hated doing that."

I am reminded of how many men Huck has had to bury, or leave where they were killed, in the past few months.

More than most men see in a lifetime, and far more than he should have had to.

Huck goes on and tells Tom about the new camp, about Chavez, and about how maybe there will be more men coming, looking for me. He tells him everything he heard at the meeting last night, except the part about Tom's dad asking if Huck should even be there. He tells Tom about my rides around town, and the boys decide then and there to go to the creek every day after school and look for tracks. I can tell Tom is excited about that—it has to be hard on him that Huck has had so many adventures in the past week and that he wasn't a part of any of them. But what Huck doesn't tell Tom is that he killed one of the men. He doesn't say anything about watching him die, and he doesn't say anything about maybe having the shot the horse. I don't say anything to Sophie, not wanting to risk the boys hearing us, but I'm sure she noticed the same thing.

Huck starts to tell Tom more about camping with the Weeminuche and hunting with the Indians. Tom remembers them from when they visited last fall, and again, we can hear in his voice how desperately he wishes he had gone. My mind drifts, and I think about how I feel kind of bad listening to Huck this way. But I guess it's a good way to learn a little about what Huck's thinking, though I wonder how I'll be able to talk about it without him knowing we both sat quietly and listened.

Both that worry and the quiet end when Sophie suddenly stands up, looks at me and says, loud enough for the boys to hear, loud enough for the boys to hear if they were at the livery instead of on the front porch, "Our son was attacked by a bear?!"

In all the excitement of what's happened in the last couple of days, I simply had forgotten about the bear, but I now see that was another in a series of mistakes. As I start to respond, Huck and Tom come racing through the door. Huck is clearly upset at both of us. He stares for a moment, then turns, and as quickly as he came in, he's back out the door and he and Tom are running toward the creek. Sophie starts to call him back, but I stop her.

"Nothing's gonna happen to him at the creek. Let him go."

Without a word, Sophie turns and walks to the stove. I'm sure she's upset about Huck. It's fairly clear she's upset with me. And she's probably upset with herself for blurting out about the bear and letting Huck know we'd been listening.

Huck, clearly angry with me, disappears into the trees by the creek, and as I'm trying to figure out what to do next, I see Ray walking the last little bit to the house. He walks up the steps, walks in the front door, which is still wide open where Huck left it, looks around, and with the practiced eye of a man who'd been married a long time to the woman who raised Sophie, knows right away I'm in trouble. He looks at me, shakes his head with a "This isn't good, but I'm glad it's not me" smile, turns back out the door and walks to the barn, suddenly—and conveniently—seeming to think of a lot of things that need fixing.

As I'm looking at Sophie, realizing that, for the first time, I've managed to disappoint or anger both her and Huck at the same time, I know I can't wait any longer to talk to Huck and will have to make things right with Sophie later tonight.

"Sophie, I'm heading down to the creek to talk to Huck. I don't know how long we'll be."

She turns, tears streaming down her face, walks over and holds me. Without a word, she turns back to the stove, so I grab my gun and Huck's coat and head to the creek. It doesn't take long to find the boys—they aren't talking much, but they've started a small fire that is easy to see. I walk up and take a seat, across from Huck and Tom. Huck starts right away.

"Why'd you listen?"

"Huck, we didn't mean to listen, but once you started talking, we just did. Probably wasn't right, and like so many things in the past couple of days, it was something I didn't plan, and maybe there was a better way."

Huck, hanging on to his anger, doesn't answer.

"Huck, I'm sorry. I'm sorry we listened to you and Tom, and I'm sorry about what happened at camp. But mostly, I'm sorry that for the last couple of days, I haven't talked to you about what happened. I thought I was doing the right thing, letting you think about it some. It's what I'd do. But maybe I do that because I don't have a dad, and maybe I do it because I'm not thirteen. But I was wrong."

I can see Huck letting go of a little of that anger, and I'm hopeful we'll be able to talk.

"Tom, I think it'd be a good idea for you to head back home. Stop by the livery and make sure everything's OK first, please. And Tom, if it's OK with your folks, maybe come back tonight after dinner, have a little pie and stay till morning?"

Tom looks at Huck. They both smile, and with a quick "yessir," he's gone.

I watch Tom head toward town and turn back to see Huck poking the fire with a stick. The sun's starting to drop and so is the temperature, so I toss Huck his coat. He slips it on, leaves it unbuttoned and goes back to poking the fire.

"Huck, I wish there was a way I could make this easy on you."

He keeps looking at the fire.

"I don't just mean the last couple of days. I mean with losing your dad, with Kurt and his men, with having to bury Payne—I mean with everything."

Huck looks up, his eyes dry and his anger gone, but not the confusion, and certainly not the pain. I slowly get up, walk the couple of steps to Huck, sit down next to him on the log, pick up a stick and start poking the fire. After a few minutes, I reach out and pull him closer to me, putting my arm around his shoulder, and kiss the top of his head.

We sit for a few more minutes. After a bit, without looking up, he just says, "Why?"

I don't know for sure what he means, or maybe I know exactly what he means. But Huck and I spend the next couple of hours, until well past dark, talking. We talk about what it was like when his dad died, when he buried Payne after Kurt's men had shot and killed him, how scared he was when he went looking for me in the mountains, and what it felt like in the alley when he tried to shoot one of Kurt's men. We talk about Frank, about killing Miguel, about probably shooting a horse. We talk about him living with me and Ray and Sophie.

I do my best to listen, and when I talk, I tell him everything. I tell him how I've felt after I've killed men, how much I miss the trail, and how much I love him and his mom. I tell him how all the planning in the world can't stand up to what life can throw at us and how, sometimes, bad things just happen.

I'm not sure I've given him the answers he needed to hear, but I've given him all of the answers I have. I listened as long as he wanted to talk, and I promised him that I'd always be there and that I'd be there sooner than I was this time. And when we both were done, since it turned out I needed to talk as much as he did, we were both exhausted. We haven't fixed everything—maybe that just can't be done—but we tried.

And as we start walking back toward the house, my arm still around his shoulders, I realize that for the first time I feel like Huck's dad, his real dad.

Scott Harris

Fourteen - Dusty Rose

Wednesdays were usually pretty quiet at the Dusty Rose. Will was cleaning and restocking the bar and thinking about how quickly he had come to look forward to his daily rides with Brock. The rides had been uneventful, but the time together had solidified their friendship. It had been a long time since Will had had a true friendship—and he valued this one. He'd settled down in Dry Springs like he had in no place before. With the new church done and ready for services starting Sunday, Will reflected on his saloon having been the town church for the past few months. It took a bit of work to turn the saloon into a church every Sunday morning, and then more work to convert it back to a saloon after services, but he smiled as he thought about how much he would actually miss it. He looked forward to being with everyone else in town for Reverend Matt's first sermon this Sunday and then the two weddings: Brock and Sophie, and Cisco and Maria. It promised to be a great day.

Will looked around the saloon and saw the usual midweek crowd, with a single exception of a new face sitting quietly alone at a small table with his back to the wall. He made a mental note to introduce himself to the man when he finished restocking, in part because it was a good idea as the owner to meet his customers, and in part because of what happened to Frank.

As Dusty sat alone at his small table, he felt Will's watchful eyes but didn't look up to meet them. He'd ridden back into Dry Springs from Santa Fe that afternoon. He was tired from over a week of almost constant riding but wanted just one drink before he walked across the street to the Soft Beds and tested the name, hopefully for a good long time. He and Will both turned toward the front when the batwings opened and five vaqueros walked in. They glanced around the saloon, looking friendly enough, and while four of them pushed two tables together, pretty close to Dusty, the fifth one walked up to the bar and ordered a bottle and six glasses, offering one to Will.

Will smiled, accepted the glass and said, "Thanks."

Dusty noticed that only two of the vaqueros were armed, which wasn't unusual, since not all vaqueros, or cowboys, carry guns, but after a lifetime riding the trails, it was still automatic for Dusty to check. Still watching the four men set up, Dusty heard Will introduce himself to the man buying the bottle, who was one of the two armed men.

"Nice to meet you, Will. I'm Luis Sanchez. We just rode in today, pushing a little over a hundred head. Boss says this is as far as we're going to go, so me and the boys left those cattle up in a little canyon outside of town and thought we'd wash away a little of the trail dust and explore town a bit."

Will nodded and asked, "You ridin' out in the morning?"

"No, señor. When I said the boss said this is as far as we're going to go, I meant we're staying."

Dusty shifted his attention away from the vaqueros and to the conversation between Will and the man he now knew was Luis.

"Settin' up a ranch around here?" Will asked, as he finished his drink and started again putting away clean glasses.

"Yep. That little canyon won't work, but it'll hold 'em for a couple of days while the boss finds some property. Said he knows someone up this way and once he takes care of some business with him, we'll start building."

"Well, Luis, welcome to Dry Springs. This first bottle's on me. Hope to see a lot of you in town and at the Dusty Rose. By the way, what's your boss's name?"

"Chavez. Francisco Chavez."

Instantly, Dusty was completely alert and completely focused. Keeping his eyes on Luis, he did notice that there was no change among the other four men, that the mention of their boss's name didn't seem to mean much to them at all. But it meant everything to Dusty. Will, not as good of a card player as Dusty, wasn't able to keep the surprise off of his face, which Luis caught, but he didn't see any reason for it, so he didn't react.

Luis thanked Will for the bottle and headed back to the tables, taking a seat, completely unaware of the impact the name Francisco Chavez was having on Will and Dusty.

As the two men processed what they had just heard, the batwings opened and Brock and Matt walked in, laughing easily, the way friends do. Brock quickly saw that there were new people, and shifting to his role as sheriff, he walked over to the vaqueros to introduce himself. Matt kept walking to the bar, intending to buy a glass for himself and one for Brock.

Will, seeing no way to stop Brock without possibly making things worse, reached quietly under the bar and placed one hand on his 12-gauge. And while Will didn't notice him do it, or have any reason to think he might, Dusty dropped his right hand below the table, slipped the thong off the hammer and set his hand on his revolver. At the same time, he shifted his chair, just slightly, but enough to let him stand easily and quickly and be facing directly at the vaqueros, should it be necessary.

Brock, having noted almost automatically that only two of the vaqueros were armed, put his left hand on the back of one of the armed vaqueros' chair and, facing the other armed man, offered his hand and his name.

"Good evening, gentlemen. I'm Brock Clemons, the sheriff here in Dry Springs."

Will nodded Matt out of the way and started to pull up the 12-gauge, and at the same time, Dusty started to stand—both expecting trouble.

But there was none. No reaction at all from any of the vaqueros, other than typical saloon politeness.

Luis, clearly the leader, was the first to reach out and shake Brock's hand, and each of the other men offered their hands as well, along with smiles and their names. Both Will and Dusty were shocked again to see that the men had not reacted at all to the name Brock Clemons. Dusty, who made a living reading men's faces, had been watching closely when Brock introduced himself and was certain the name meant nothing to any of the vaqueros.

Will relaxed, a bit, as did Dusty and Brock, who, having assured himself there was no trouble with the vaqueros, excused himself and walked up to the bar. Matt, not knowing why Will had moved him away, but knowing what he kept under the bar, started to ask questions. Will waited a moment for Brock and then told them both what he had learned from Sanchez—that these vaqueros had driven a hundred or so head of cattle into the area with plans to set up a ranch, and more importantly, that their boss was Francisco Chavez and that it appeared all these men knew about what was happening was that their boss had some business to clear up with someone in town.

Brock and Matt understood instantly what that "business" was and also knew right away, based on the men's non-reaction to meeting Brock, that they had no idea who the business was with, or what the business was. Still sitting by himself, Dusty had reached the same conclusions, though he did keep his hand resting on the butt of his gun.

Brock lowered his voice so the vaqueros couldn't hear, which meant that Dusty couldn't either, and explained to Will that he and Matt had crossed the tracks of the cattle and about ten riders. They'd followed the trail to the opening of Coyote Canyon, but since it was getting late and Brock wasn't expecting that Chavez would show up with a herd of cattle, he dismissed it as a non-threat and they turned back to town. Brock explained that he'd planned on he and Will riding out to talk to the newcomers on their morning ride tomorrow, but obviously, they needed a new plan.

At the same time, Dusty was listening to the vaqueros as they talked among themselves.

Vic Tejada, who was the other armed one, said, "I don't know why Chavez has Diego and those other two men with him. They never do any work, staying to themselves, sitting around playing cards. And except for chow, they never have anything to do with us. Wouldn't even help with the cattle tonight. Had to leave Juan behind to keep the cattle bottled up in that canyon."

A couple of the other vaqueros, Benito Juarez and Jose de Herrera, sounded their agreement. They, like the others, had come over to Chavez's ranch with the cattle when he bought his first herd. They'd always felt they worked more for Miguel and Luis than they did for Chavez, though like all good vaqueros, as long as they were drawing pay, they rode for the brand. One of the other vaqueros, Roberto Silva, brought up that Miguel had been gone now for a couple of weeks and, for the couple of months before that, had been spending more time with Chavez and Diego and less time with the cattle. Again, everyone nodded in agreement, but none of them had an explanation to offer.

Dusty had heard enough and slowly stood up, walking the short distance to the vaqueros' table. His hand was off of his gun, but hung low and ready if he needed it. Will, Matt and Brock saw him move but had been focused on their own conversation, so they'd heard nothing of what the vaqueros were saying. They kept talking to each other as Dusty introduced himself to the vaqueros, noticing that his name elicited no reaction, the same as Brock's. One of the men started to get up and get Dusty a chair, but he politely declined, saying he preferred to remain standing for their conversation. The way he said it, while not threatening, drew everyone's attention, and Dusty noted that Vic, who was seated directly across from him, dropped his hand and scooted his chair back, just a bit.

"Gentlemen, you don't know me. But your boss does, and I know him. And unfortunately, that creates a problem for all of us. Please forgive me for listening in on your conversation, but having done so, the good news is I am convinced that not only are you not involved in this situation except that you work for Chavez, but you are also completely unaware of the nature of the problem."

Vic, his blood starting to boil a little, said, "You mention a problem. What problem are you talking about?"

"I will explain it to you, but it's going to take a few minutes to do so. At the end of my explanation, you will each have a decision to make. I hope to explain things to you in a way that allows you to make the right decision."

The five men looked at each other, and then Luis gave Dusty a nod, encouraging him to continue. None of the men relaxed, but they were all paying attention.

"You probably noticed that about two weeks ago, eight men from Chavez's ranch left—I am assuming without explanation, then or now."

The looks from the vaqueros confirmed that they knew.

"Those men, including Miguel, who I heard you mention, were sent in two groups of four to kill two men. One of those men was me. None of them will be returning, something your boss is probably just now learning."

Dusty saw Vic tense up and knew he was considering going for his gun. Dusty drew his, far faster than any of the vaqueros would have suspected from a man who looked so weak and tired, and pointed it at Vic.

"Please don't do that."

Vic didn't draw, but didn't move his hand either. When it came to standing up for the brand, Vic was always the first and the strongest, but some of what the man was saying made sense, and he did have a gun pointed directly at his chest. Sitting next to Vic was Benito Juarez. Without moving the gun, Dusty spoke to Juarez.

"Mr. Juarez, please reach slowly into Mr. Tejada's holster and pull his gun out, handing it to Mr. Sanchez."

Benito looked at Vic, who nodded and very reluctantly allowed his gun to be taken and given to Luis.

"Mr. Tejada, I understand your anger and your loyalty to the brand. I respect both. However, I believe when I am done explaining what has happened, and what your boss intends to happen, you'll understand me and perhaps change your position."

With that, Dusty flipped his own gun and, holding onto the barrel, handed it to Luis butt first.

"However, when I'm done, if you are still not satisfied, I'll ask Mr. Sanchez to return our weapons, and the two of us will step outside of the bar, which I'm sure the bartender will appreciate, and settle our differences. Is this agreeable?"

Vic couldn't see the downside to listening, and since he also couldn't help but notice how quickly Dusty had drawn his weapon, he agreed to the terms.

Dusty then spent the next few minutes telling the men how Sheriff Dean, who they all knew, or knew of, had explained to him what had happened to Chavez—how he'd lost his ranch and stolen the hundred cattle from Dan Pulos, another name the men knew. He then went on to explain that Chavez had tried to have two men killed, two men he apparently blamed for his problems, Dusty being one of them. Though he didn't say who the second target was, he did let them know that all eight of the men Chavez had sent had been killed, including Miguel. He went on and explained how he, along with many others, had won quite a bit of money from Chavez playing poker over the last year or so, and it had reached the point where he could no longer pay his debts. Dusty told the men he thought that was why he was a target, but he didn't know about the other man.

Vic, a man who valued loyalty and for close to thirty years had always ridden for the brand he worked for, was not ready to take Dusty's story at face value.

"How do we know what you're saying is true?"

Dusty waited for a moment before answering. "You don't." He let that sink in.

"But, let me ask you. How else would you explain what's happened, and why you're sitting here now? Where did the eight men go, and why haven't they come back? Why would Chavez leave his family hacienda and most of his cattle and people behind? Why would he have hired gun hands, and why would they be riding with him now? And last, if it's not true, what do I have to gain by telling you this?"

Dusty stopped talking and watched the five men, knowing this was the moment where they would either accept what he knew to be the truth or it would turn violent. Part of him wished he hadn't handed his gun to Sanchez, but he trusted his instincts. The men didn't speak, but looked around at each other, and finally, they were all looking to Luis.

Luis took a deep breath, turned to Dusty and said, "If this is all true, what do you suggest we do next?"

Dusty breathed a huge sigh of relief, turned back to his table, picked up his unfinished glass of bourbon, grabbed a chair and sat down with the vaqueros. He reached into his pocket slowly, knowing Vic was still on edge, and pulled out a single sheet of paper. He handed it to Luis.

To whom it may concern,

I, Dan Pulos, as the sole owner of what has previously been known as the Rancho del Cielo, including all of its cattle, hereby acknowledge selling approximately 100 head of cattle, known to be branded with the slashRC brand, current whereabouts not known, to Mr. Dusty Stevens for $1.

It was dated the previous Friday, signed by Dan Pulos, and witnessed by Jeremy Binns and Sheriff Geoff Dean.

Luis read the note, looked up at Dusty and passed the note around. For the benefit of those who couldn't read, or at least couldn't read English, Benito read it aloud. Dusty could tell by their faces that they believed him. He then shared his plan.

"Since you clearly have nothing to do with what's been happening, I am going to sell you those cattle for one dollar and give you the receipt tonight. You're going to head back to the canyon and move those cattle somewhere else by the end of the day tomorrow. And Friday morning, I'm riding into that canyon and will kill everyone who's still there."

The men couldn't have been much more surprised, but they weren't any more surprised than Brock was. Dusty had been so focused on the vaqueros that he hadn't noticed that it had gotten quiet at the bar and that Will, Matt and Brock had heard the tail end of the conversation. Before Dusty could continue, the three men walked over.

Without any further introductions, Brock looked directly at Dusty and said, "I heard what you said, at least the last part, and I have plenty of questions for you—as well as for you men." He looked around the table. "But you won't be riding out Friday morning to kill anyone."

Dusty looked up at Brock and said, "We both know who those men are, what they have done and what they are planning to do."

"You're right, but I'm the sheriff here in Dry Springs, so that makes it my job."

Dusty continued to look straight at Brock. "It's my job too."

"Why?"

"Because you're my son."

Fifteen - Brock

I'm not sure what answer I was expecting when I asked, "Why?" But learning that this man is my father certainly wasn't it. I've spent more than two years of my life looking for him, my entire life without him, and now that I've found him, or I guess, he's found me, I have no idea what to say.

Dusty keeps talking. "Gentlemen, you've met the sheriff, but what you don't know is that he is the second man I told you about that Chavez is trying to kill. I believe killing him is the 'business' your boss mentioned that he plans to take care of. I don't believe he knows I'm here, but he will find out, and when he does, it will only get worse."

As I'm trying to figure out how he knows this, I remember back to the town meeting last week and the man I didn't know, but felt like I should. It hits me now that this is the same man. I don't know where he's been since then, or the past twenty years, but it is clear he's involved in what's happening. I still don't know what to say, but he does.

"Brock, I think it would be a good idea for you, and the men with you, to pull up some chairs, and we'll discuss what's going to happen next."

And we do.

No sooner are we all seated than Cisco and Clybs walk in the front door, looking for friends and a drink. Both men see Will, Matt and me and start to walk over. By the time they get to the table, Cisco recognizes the vaqueros and they obviously recognize him. The vaqueros, who have been hit by surprise after surprise tonight, embrace this one and warmly welcome Cisco. It's clear from Cisco's reaction that these are friends of his—and good men. Introductions are made all the way around. Will and Matt grab a couple of bottles and plenty of glasses from the bar, and soon there are eleven of us sitting around the gathered tables. Conveniently, we are the only ones remaining in the saloon.

Since all of us at the tables are involved, at various levels, it makes sense to bring everyone up to date on what has happened the last few months. Cisco starts by telling everyone what happened back at Rancho del Cielo when Chavez tried to steal everything, and then what happened last week when we were ambushed by Miguel and the others, which probably removes any lingering doubts the vaqueros—even Vic—may have had about Chavez and his involvement.

I already know all of this, so my mind drifts to what is huge news for me—I'm sitting at a table with my father! Dusty shares about the Santa Fe gambling and Chavez's huge losses and goes over again what he learned last week on his trip back to Santa Fe, including how he came to own the cattle. When Cisco and Dusty are done, having covered most of my involvement, I have very little to add—still reeling as I sit across the table from my father—though everyone else seems to have questions about some part of what's happened.

But, after an hour or so, the stories all told, questions asked and answered, and everyone at the table in agreement as to what has happened, it's time to discuss what's going to happen next. And that's my job.

"Gentlemen, there have been quite a few surprises in the last couple of hours", I look directly at Dusty, smiling, "for all of us. I don't know if there are any more coming, but for me, I hope that's all there is for tonight."

There is shared laughter around the table, reflecting the truth of my statement and how comfortable the men have become with each other as the hours have passed, stories have been told and bottles have been killed.

Addressing the vaqueros, I ask, "Do any of you have any doubts about what's been shared here tonight?"

When it's clear they don't, I ask the tougher question. "I agree with what Dusty suggested earlier, about you buying the cattle from him and moving them out of Coyote Canyon tomorrow. I've played in the same poker games as Dusty. I've played with Pulos and Binns and spent time with Sheriff Dean. I have no doubts left about what Dusty said. However, for you, this means leaving Chavez and leaving the brand. Are you willing to do that?"

I know that any cowboy, or vaquero, worth his saddle rides for the brand, almost always for better or worse. There is an honor among those who work cattle, a pride in what they do and, when possible, those they do it for. Thousands of bar fights have started when a cowboy feels his brand has been insulted or challenged, and range wars are not uncommon between the brands, with all hands fighting. Leaving a brand is never taken lightly by the men who take pride in their own names. But murder and cattle rustling are two things that no good man, vaquero or not, can condone.

This time, the men all look to Vic and even though I can tell it's painful for him, he says, "Sí, we will do what has been suggested."

Relieved, I ask, "Do you see any problems moving the cattle tomorrow?"

113

Luis answers, "No. But I do not know where is the best place to move them."

I think for a moment, and then the answer is obvious. "Just south of Coyote Canyon—that's where you have them now—is Frank's ranch. Frank's the man who was killed by Miguel and the other men. You rode through it on your way to the canyon. And I think for now, and permanently, should you choose to stay in Dry Springs, that will be the perfect place."

We talk about this for a while, with Cisco sharing with his old friends how great it is to live in Dry Springs and how the town is growing. The vaqueros, who had already planned to settle here when they rode in with Chavez, quickly agree to stay. I explain to them that once they've settled in on Frank's ranch and I've taken care of Chavez and his men, I'll introduce them to Thurm, the town banker, and they can buy the ranch. They laugh when I say it will be a little more than a dollar, but they say they have some money, and I assure them Thurm will be willing to work with them and take payments. I tell them how all the money will be going to Frank's family in Guatemala.

At this, Luis stands and raises his glass. "To Frank—who we never met, but all knew. May he rest in peace with his father and his family in Guatemala, and may we honor him in the way we run our new ranch, which I propose we name the barFbar in his honor."

The vaqueros are the first to raise their glasses, but we all stand and join in with a shout. We drink a toast to Frank, then to the new ranch—the barFbar—and another to new friends. But then, remembering what happened last week when there were too many toasts, I suggest that maybe we all have plenty to do and need to be at our best.

Everyone agrees, and while Will and Matt cap what little is left in the bottles and return them to the bar, coming back to the tables with cigars for all, Dusty, who hasn't said a word since I started talking, speaks up.

"What about Chavez and his men?"

I've been thinking about that myself. Before answering, I accept a cigar from Matt, clip the end and take a moment to light it. Others are doing the same, though not Dusty, and all have their eyes on me. I take a good long draw, the first one always being my favorite, and look around the table.

"I'll be riding out there Friday morning to arrest those men."

There is an immediate reaction as everyone at the table is offering, insisting, to go with me.

I look first at the vaqueros. "Gentlemen, you will have plenty to do on Friday—and for a while—settling your cattle in, starting to build your ranch, laying in supplies and everything else necessary for your move. Plus, it is enough that are you leaving the brand. It is too much—and not necessary—to ask you to turn around and ride against it."

Cisco looks at Luis and the other men and tells them I am right, that it is the right thing to do. This is perfect for me, because it allows me to next do what I need to do and what I know Cisco won't like.

"Cisco, I am glad you feel this way, because I want you to ride with these men."

He immediately turns to me and begins protesting. I put a hand on his shoulder to stop him.

"I know you want to ride Friday. But you are the only one who knows these men, knows cattle, and knows Frank's ranch, including where the water is. It is better if you help them. If Chavez and his men get past me, they'll come looking for these men and the cattle, and they'll need someone with them who knows their way around. That's you, Cisco."

He understands and reluctantly agrees, and then Clybs, who's been pretty quiet all night, jumps in.

"They won't get past us, Brock." I have really grown fond of Clybs these past few months and have enjoyed watching him grow up. He's a good senior deputy, but I still don't think he's ready for what might happen Friday.

"Clybs, I'm going to need you to stay here. The town needs a sheriff, and again, if something happens to me, Chavez and his men will be riding into town, and I need you to take care of it. We'll talk tomorrow about how you can be ready for that."

Like Cisco, Clybs reluctantly agrees with me, but he's very clearly not happy about it.

Lined up next are Matt and Will. They look at each other and then back at me, and Matt says, "We're riding with you."

I start to tell them why they can't, but this time it's me who's interrupted and shut down.

Will makes it clear he won't take no for an answer. "Brock, you made us deputies for a reason. And I ain't been riding around this town every day just for the pony ride. I understand why Cisco should ride with these good men and why you need our senior deputy to stay in town, but you know there's no good reason why Matt and I can't ride with you."

I still feel this is my job, both personally and as sheriff, and start to say so.

Will stops me again. "Brock, we let you ride out of this town alone once before, a shame many of us carry today. I swore then—and I swear now—it's not going to happen again. You've made us deputies, so if that's what you're worried about, it's all legal. If it's anything else you're worried about, this town is just as much ours as it is yours, so these men are just as much our problem as they are yours. Now, we can ride with you or just behind you if you don't want the company, but when you ride into Coyote Canyon Friday morning, you won't be alone."

This time it's my turn to silently agree, unable to argue and grateful for their friendship. Also, I know I can't do anything to stop them.

I had almost forgot about Dusty, my father, the man who started all of this tonight.

"I'll be riding out Friday morning as well. Be obliged if I could ride with you."

I look at him. "I understand your wanting to go. But we're riding out there to arrest these men, not to kill them. That makes it a legal matter. It'd be best if you stayed right here in Dry Springs."

Dusty looks around the table, stopping for just a moment at each of the other nine men, before turning back to me.

"We both know, we all know, those men aren't going to allow themselves to be arrested. And once you're done trying, the only way this ends is with shooting. You also know he's tried to kill me too, which makes it personal. I've made a lot of mistakes in my life, some of which I hope to talk to you about, but I've never let another man fight my battles for me—and it's not going to start now."

I make one last effort. "Dusty, this is a legal matter. Deputies only."

"Well, Sheriff, I plan on riding out to Coyote Canyon Friday morning, so you better arrest me or deputize me."

Sixteen - Brock

And with that, for the moment, the conversation stops. I keep looking at Dusty but can feel the other nine men looking at me. After a very long moment, I look around at the other men.

"We all have plenty to do tomorrow. Cisco, I suggest you meet these men about a mile or so south of Coyote Canyon. Better not to raise any suspicions by having Chavez and his gunmen see any new faces, especially yours. If it's OK, I'll ride out with you and help get things started at Frank's."

Everyone quickly agrees. Will and Matt both want to ride with us, but I ask them to stay here in case Chavez, or any of his men, show up and Clybs needs any help. All that's left is to talk to Dusty. I hadn't realized how long we'd all been talking or how late it had gotten, and I now remember I haven't been home yet and Sophie doesn't know where I am. I turn to Dusty.

"I've got to head up to the house and let the family know I'm OK. Care to walk with me?"

He grabs his coat off the back of his chair and slips it on, and we walk out the door along with everyone else, except Will, who stays behind to close up. Plans are confirmed, goodbyes are said, hands are shaken and then everyone is gone, leaving Dusty and me standing alone in front of the Dusty Rose. Without a word, I start toward the house, and Dusty joins me. When we get to the porch, I ask him to wait while I go inside. Ray and Huck are asleep, but Sophie is up, reading, or at least holding, a book, in front of the fire. I smile, walk over and give her a kiss.

"Sophie, there's a man on the front porch. I need to…" And I stop.

She looks into my eyes. "Are you OK?"

"I think so, but I need to talk to him, and I think it's going to take a while. I want to tell you…"

"Just go. Take care of what you need to. I'm going to bed. Wake me when you're done, and we'll talk."

I thank her; grab two glasses, a bottle of bourbon and a cigar; kiss her gently on the cheek; give silent thanks for the thousandth time since we first met; and walk back out to the porch. Dusty is still standing, his back to the door, looking out over Dry Springs. I give a small cough as notice that I'm back, and he turns around. We each take a seat, and then I hand him a glass, set the bottle between us and start taking my time with the cigar.

"I noticed earlier you don't smoke."

"I've got tuberculosis. Cigars make it worse." A night already filled with surprises chooses now to add a huge one. "The bourbon doesn't help either, but a man needs to hold onto at least one vice, even if things get a little tough. Maybe especially when they get a little tough."

And that's how a conversation more than twenty years in the making, and more than two years rehearsed in my head, begins. I finally meet my father—and he's dying. He pours himself a healthy glass and scoots the bottle back toward me. I stop working on my cigar, hold it up and ask, "This OK with you?"

"Yeah, I still like the smell. I just can't inhale deep anymore. Used to be one of my favorite things on the trail, at the end of the day. Nice fire, something to eat, a beautiful sunset and a good cigar."

Taking a page from Sophie's book, I turn so I'm looking right at him and ask, "Why now?"

Without looking up from his bourbon, he says, "Because I'm dying."

I guess I knew when he said tuberculosis, but to hear it said so calmly, so matter-of-factly, is almost eerie. He keeps right on talking.

"I haven't done much in my life I regret, but the way I treated your mom and the way I treated you has been a pretty heavy load to carry. Even now, I have to admit I first came to Dry Springs for me, not for you. I figured I wanted to meet you before I died. Didn't even know about Sophie or Huck. But over the past couple of weeks, all that's changed."

He coughs, violently, and this time I notice a little blood as he wipes his mouth with his handkerchief. I don't say anything—I don't know what to say. So I wait, and he starts again.

"Even if it were somehow possible, I don't have enough time left to become a father to you. But if you'd allow me, I'd like to get to know you—and Sophie and Huck—and maybe you could get to know me a little bit too. If you don't want that, I understand, but so that we're clear, it doesn't change me riding out with you Friday morning."

I take a sip of bourbon and use relighting my cigar, which I hadn't touched while he was talking, as an excuse for not looking directly at him and to give me a little time to think. This isn't just about me, but also about Sophie, Huck and even Ray. Dusty seems like a good man, honest about his mistakes and his hopes, and maybe we should let him into our lives.

I look up, the cigar relit, and see he's refilled both our glasses.

"Tell me about mom."

Dusty spends the next few hours telling me all the stories I wanted to hear, and maybe a couple I didn't. He tells me how they met and fell in love, how he really hoped that London would work and why it didn't, how hard it was to leave her—and me—and how he wrestled with traveling back to London time after time, coming close one time, even making it as far as New York.

He tells me stories of living on the trail for more than twenty years and the people he's met—those he's befriended and those he's killed—the adventures he's had, the places he's been and the changes he's seen.

He slows down a bit when he gets to the last couple of years. He talks about how when he took sick he had to switch to gambling just to survive, but tells me it isn't that bad of a life. He also tells me how bad he felt when he knew I was looking for him and even about the night in Denver when he sat at the table next to me, but didn't say anything. And then he talks about how he did quite a bit of gambling in Santa Fe and what happened with him and Chavez. How Chavez cheated, but poorly, and how he took advantage of that to win quite a bit of money from him.

Finally, we get to the part where he first rode into Dry Springs, but it is obvious that he's exhausted and hurting.

"Dusty, let's call it a night. I've got a long day tomorrow, including swearing you in as a deputy." He looks up, with a smile. "And we both have a tough day coming Friday. Let's have dinner here tomorrow night, after I get back from Frank's ranch and helping the vaqueros, and I'll introduce you to Sophie, Huck and Ray."

He smiles at that and again when I offer for him to stay the night at the house. But he says he already has a room at the Soft Beds, his stuff is there and he needs to stretch his legs after sitting for so long.

I shake his hand and watch him walk slowly down the hill toward town. I watch until he is out of sight and then stand just looking at the stars and thinking. I turn as the door opens. There stands Sophie. She'd gone to bed hours ago— I noticed when she blew the lantern out—but somehow she knew Dusty had left, and she was checking on me.

I walk over and take her in my arms—in part because it had grown chilly and she wasn't dressed for it, and in part because I needed to. After a bit, we go back into the house and close the door against the cold. I take her hand and walk her to her bedroom, actually stepping inside for the very first time. I tuck her in and sit on the edge of the bed, nervous and comfortable at the same time.

"Sophie, that was my father."

She squeezes my hand. "You talked for a long time."

And with that, it all spills out. I tell her everything we talked about on the porch and then everything that happened and was talked about at the Dusty Rose. I tell her what I need to do tomorrow and, finally, what I need to do Friday. She doesn't say a word the entire time. She just holds my hand, looks into my eyes and listens.

When I'm done, the first thing she wants to talk about is Friday.

"Is there any other way?"

"Sophie, you know there isn't. After what Chavez has already done, we both know he didn't ride all the way here to make peace. I have to do it for us, or we'll never rest easy, and I have to do it as the sheriff of Dry Springs. I don't feel good about Matt and Will coming, but I don't have much choice."

She seems to accept that and asks, "What about Dusty?"

I stop for a moment and look around the room, noticing that a hint of light is creeping in, which means we've talked from whenever to dawn. It also means I need to leave soon to meet Cisco and the vaqueros. And last, it means that between the bourbon last night and no sleep, it's going to be a long day.

"Do you mean about Friday, or about being my father."

"Both."

"I'm going to deputize him today and let him ride with us Friday. I don't even know if I mean 'let him.' I can't stop him from riding out there. He hasn't done anything I could arrest him for. And he's right—he's in this as much as

I am. They tried to kill him too. I know I'd have to go if I were him. He told me some things tonight." I stop and look away, thinking of some of the things he went through, some of the stories he told me tonight about riding alone in the territory all these years.

"I know he'll be able to handle himself."

"And what about him as your father?"

I don't know. I just don't know. I start telling Sophie, as much as I understand it, what it feels like to meet him after all this time. How it makes me wonder even more what it would have been like to have a father. The confusion of liking him, but still being unable to understand how he could have left me and my mother, how he could have stayed away my entire life, and then, how he could have avoided me when he knew I was looking for him. I tell her how much it hurt when he told me he sat at a poker table next to me, knowing who I was, and calmly stood up, cashed in his chips and rode away without a word.

Sophie still doesn't say anything as I tell her how concerned I am about how him being in our life might impact our family. I share the thoughts I've been having about how we are just getting used to each other, to Huck, and how I've grown to think of her father as kind of mine. I wonder aloud whether allowing him into our life be better for all of us. And then, having forgotten to say anything about it earlier, I tell her how he is dying and how, after all the disappointment, I'm not sure I'm ready to allow myself to get to know him and then lose him again.

Spent, physically and emotionally, I lay my head on Sophie's chest, and she just holds me. After a couple of minutes, quietly, she says, "You know we'll be fine. I would like to get to know him, and you know Huck would love to know his other grandfather. Thank you for being concerned about my dad, but I promise you, if you allow it, he'll welcome Dusty into our home. As a guest if you want, or as a part of the family."

I sit back up and tell her how perfect I think our family is right now. How I'm working so hard to learn how to be a sheriff, a father and a husband and how I wonder if this is the right time to add such a serious complication.

"Brock, I love you—and Huck and my dad. But there are no perfect families, and it's impossible to protect all of us from everything. This might be messy, and maybe it doesn't turn out for the best, but you already know that you can't turn him away."

I think what about she's said. "I know you're right, and I know we'll be OK and your dad will be OK. But what about Huck? He's been through so much. To bring Dusty into his life, knowing he'll be dying soon, is that the right thing to do?"

"Brock, even if it's only for a little while, and even if it hurts, we can't deny him getting to know Dusty. Look what it did to you when you found out your dad was alive and your mom had been lying to you, even if she thought it was for the best. Do you want to do the same thing to Huck with his grandfather?"

As I'm thinking about this, still unsure but knowing I have to leave to meet Cisco, she says one final thing.

"I know you're worried about us, and I know you're upset at what he's done—and hasn't done—for the past twenty years, but he's here now, he's trying and he doesn't have very much time left."

She sits up, takes both my hands in hers, kisses me on the cheek and says, "Brock, this may or may not be fair, but your dad needs a son as much as Huck needed a father."

Seventeen - Sophie

Sophie was glad she had decided to close the school today and tomorrow. She had done it at the insistence of her friends, who said she would need the couple of extra days to get ready for her wedding. So, even though it felt very indulgent, even selfish, she allowed herself to be talked into it. But now, there was so much more that was happening, some of which she was scared about, some of which she still didn't know how she felt about, and some of which she resented, at least a little. She was going to need some, if not all, of this time to sort out exactly what was happening, how she felt about it and what, if anything, she could do to help.

When she talked with Nerissa, Stacy and Kim about their weddings, everything they said happened in the few days before their weddings had been about the weddings, which Sophie knew, were mostly about the bride. While Sophie almost always thought of others before herself and had always considered herself to be very practical, she found herself getting swept away with the planning and caught herself frequently daydreaming about what the wedding day—and night—were going to be like. She loved sitting on her front porch with Maria and talking about what being married was like and dreaming about having children.

But starting with Frank's death, Brock's focus had not been on the wedding, and even though she understood, if she was honest with herself, it hurt. Even this morning, when they spent hours discussing Chavez and Dusty, who she now realized would be her father-in-law, the wedding hadn't even come up. As silly as it seemed now, she had been so excited to tell him about her wedding dress, which Maria had finished yesterday and was about the prettiest thing she had ever seen.

There was a time when having a man in her bedroom for the first time would have been significant, and maybe it was, but with everything else that was happening, she didn't give it much thought this morning. She did notice how natural it felt to have Brock there and looked forward even more to when he would be there every night. And that thought lasted less than a minute before she was drawn back to the reality of the next couple of days and how dangerous, again, they were going to be for Brock and the others.

Sophie had already made plans to meet Maria, Stacy and Kim for breakfast at Hattie's, and she decided to get up now and go down early. She needed to talk, and it wasn't anything she could talk to her dad, or Huck, about. She left them a note on the kitchen table and walked down to town to help Nerissa open Hattie's and to start to sort through her thoughts and feelings. She also knew that Maria had to be having some of the same thoughts and fears about Cisco, even though she'd been married before, and it would be good for them to be able to talk about it, and to be together.

Since Nolan and Shawn had not been at the Dusty Rose last night, she guessed that Nerissa and Kim didn't know what was happening, though she was almost certain that Stacy and Maria would, since Cisco and Matt were not only there but were going to be very involved in whatever happened over the next two days. It was going to be another hour before the other girls came by, so Sophie spent that hour discussing the wedding, the restaurant and kids with Nerissa. When Nerissa started telling her stories about what Oscar and Hattie had been up to the last couple of days, she even managed to forget everything else, at least for a little while.

But that changed the moment Maria walked in the door, wearing the same look Sophie figured she had on her own face. No one was more surprised than Nerissa when Maria and Sophie fell into each other's arms, crying.

Kim and Stacy were only minutes behind, and as the story started to unfold, Nerissa decided her friends needed her and the town could go one morning without Hattie's being open. So, she walked over to the front window, flipped the sign to Closed and drew the shades. Nolan walked out of the kitchen to see what was happening, and Nerissa, with only a look, let him know it was time for him to be somewhere else. Confused about wht, but clear on what was expected, he backed into the kitchen and wasn't seen again that morning.

The girls spent the next couple of hours just talking, bringing each other up to date on what was happening with them and their families and how it was being impacted by the sudden appearance of Chavez and his men. And though Dusty showing up would mostly impact Sophie and her family, they all wanted to talk about it.

They weren't disturbed once, which wouldn't have been surprising had they known that Nolan was sitting out on the front porch with Hattie and Oscar, giving away the donuts he and Nerissa had baked that morning and letting everyone know they would be open again tomorrow morning, which, since he had no idea what was happening inside, he hoped was true. He also hoped the McClaskeys didn't come by this morning, or he knew he'd run out of donuts.

Hours passed and the girls felt better for having talked, cried and even laughed, at least a little. Maria, Stacy and Sophie all understood that their men were doing what they had to do, and they also knew they couldn't have stopped them from doing it, even if they wanted to. Maybe they had talked all they could about Chavez and Dusty, or maybe it was therapeutic to do so, but they finally found themselves talking about the weddings, which, even with everything else that was happening, was still fun.

They may have continued doing that for the rest of the afternoon, but Nolan sheepishly popped his head out of the kitchen and asked Nerissa if they were going to open for lunch. She looked around, saw that the girls really seemed to be OK, or at least as OK as they could be, and let Nolan know they would.

Everyone hugged and made plans to meet again tomorrow morning, though this time Nerissa would let Nolan open the restaurant. And with that, Sophie headed back home feeling much better—still scared, but not alone, and thankful again for the friends she had in her life.

Eighteen - Brock

I'm glad I told Cisco I'd meet him this morning south of Coyote Canyon, rather than riding out together. It's only about an hour ride out there, but as much as I enjoy Cisco's company, I need the time to think. Leaving now, even riding slow, I should still be there an hour, maybe two, before Cisco, Luis and the rest of the vaqueros, and maybe I'll be able to figure things out, or at least some of them.

I take my time with Horse, rubbing her down, giving her a little extra grain. I do the same with Spirit too, so he doesn't feel left out, and treat them both to a peppermint candy. I start to figure out that I'm just stalling, that I really just want to go back inside and spend the morning with Sophie—maybe talking all morning about everything that's happening, or maybe not saying a word, but either way, just being with her. But I'm the sheriff, and I'm being hunted, so it's my job and my responsibility to see this thing with Chavez through to the end. And part of that is riding out there this morning, making sure the vaqueros are safely away from Coyote Canyon and set up at Frank's place. Once that's done, I can ride home to Sophie and start to figure out tomorrow.

I ride into town and over to Hattie's. They're not open this early, but I know they're already up and working, so I knock on the back door. Nolan opens up, and I can tell by his face he knows everything that's happening. He shakes my hand and asks if there's anything he can do.

"There is. Actually, two things. I'm a little concerned that while Cisco and I are out with the vaqueros today, Chavez and his men may ride in. I don't expect there'll be any trouble, unless they see Dusty. He's staying right here at the hotel. When he comes down for breakfast, can you please tell him I'd like him to stay out of sight today? He won't like it, but tell him all he has to do is wait until tomorrow and we'll take care of this—together."

"Sure, easy enough. What's the other thing?"

"I figure if Chavez does ride in, the first place he and his men will stop will be across the street at the Dusty Rose. Keep your eyes open, and if they show up, go get Matt, Ray and a couple of the boys and make your way to the saloon. Again, I don't think they'll be any trouble, but I think it'd be best if Will wasn't alone."

"Will do, Sheriff. Good luck today."

"Thanks." I turn to leave, and Nerissa walks in from the dining room. She walks across the kitchen, and surprising me and Nolan, throws her arms around me and gives me a hug, something she's never done before. She whispers in my ear.

"Don't forget about Sophie and your wedding."

And without another word, she hands me a couple of donuts—which I now remember is why I stopped by in the first place—grabs some plates and heads back to the dining room. Nolan smiles and says, "I know that look. Whatever she said, she meant it."

I smile back, shaking my head, and take a bite out of a delicious, still-hot donut before I turn to leave, fresh out of reasons, or excuses, to not get going.

I've only been to Coyote Canyon once, but I easily pick up the vaqueros tracks from last night, so I know I'm heading the right way. The morning is still crisp, even cold, and when I finish the donuts, I button up my coat. I take a look around, but I don't see anyone else, including Wolf, who more and more often stays back with Huck. I'd like to think it's because Huck feeds her, even though I've asked him not to, but honestly, I think Wolf just prefers following Huck. It's good for Huck—and Wolf—but I do miss having her with me on mornings like this.

Horse is feeling strong, and I can tell she wants to run, for no other reason than that it's a beautiful morning and she wants to stretch her legs. I don't want to tire her out too much because, while I don't expect any trouble today, it's never smart to have a spent horse when you're out on the trail. You never know when the difference between life and death might be a fast horse with plenty of stamina. On the other hand, we can both use a good run, so I give her her head and she's off like a shot.

After a couple of miles, I reign her in, even though I can tell she'd like to keep running. We trot for a bit and then back off to an easy walk. After about a half hour, I figure I'm as close to Coyote Canyon as I want to go this morning, and I turn south toward Frank's place. I start thinking again about Frank's death, how senseless it was, and I find myself getting angry all over again. I wonder, depending on how things go tomorrow, if I'll ever even know why Chavez wants me dead, and so much so that he'll order the deaths of so many people. It does not seem like the act of a sane man.

I spend the next half hour trying to figure Chavez out, but I'm no closer now than I've been since it happened. I pull up to Frank's place and somehow it feels like I'm intruding. It's only been a couple of weeks since Frank was killed, but in a way, it feels like his place has been empty for years. I'm uncomfortable enough that even though it's cold I decide to wait outside for Cisco and the vaqueros. Frank had a nice pond out front, so I unsaddle Horse and let her roll, drink her fill and eat as much grass as she'd like.

There's not much for me to do, so I find myself a comfortable tree to sit against and settle in to wait. I notice a nice piece of sandstone and use it to sharpen my Bowie knife, as much to pass the time as to sharpen an already sharp blade. After a few minutes, I trade the knife for a good cigar and take my time lighting it up. Horse is done rolling and drinking, so she's enjoying the good grass that grows by the pond. I wish Wolf were here. Somehow, it's always comforting when she's with me on the trail, but she's back in Dry Springs, probably just outside of the livery, keeping an eye on Huck while he does his chores.

I remember what Nerissa said about Sophie and the wedding, and I feel even worse that we didn't talk about it at all this morning. I'm sure she wanted to, but instead, we kept talking about what was happening with me, and then I was gone. It seems in the time I've known her there have been too many crises, too many bad things happening. And now, on what should be the best week of her life—and mine— Chavez shows up to kill me, and anyone who gets in the way, and my father shows up after more than twenty years. She's already agreed to share her day with Cisco and Maria, so I can see where it might be too much to have her share it with Chavez and Dusty too.

And I guess, if I admit it to myself, she knows Chavez and his men aren't going to allow themselves to be arrested, which means there's going to be shooting, which means that some of us are going to get hurt, or killed. While I like my chances, it's not guaranteed I won't be one of them. She's already seen me get shot once, and she's probably afraid it's going to happen again. The more I think about tomorrow, the more I think it might be harder on Sophie—

waiting back at the house, not knowing what's going to happen, but knowing what could—than it will be on me.

I wish I could look past tomorrow and see Sunday and the wedding, but I can't. I know it's there and I know I want it, in large part, if I'm honest with myself, because it means I survived tomorrow, but mostly because I simply want to be married to Sophie.

I'm also starting to think about what it would be like to not be sheriff. It's crossed my mind before that in the towns I've traveled to and through there aren't a lot of old sheriffs. I hadn't put much thought to it until recently, but sheriffs do seem to attract trouble and bullets, and I've had plenty of both since I rode into Dry Springs. Just as I start to roll that around my head, I see a good-size dust cloud coming from the north, which I'm guessing is Cisco, the vaqueros and the cattle. I saddle Horse up and start riding out to meet them.

I haven't gone a mile when I see Cisco riding out front, the cattle behind with a couple of vaqueros on each side and two more trailing. I ride up, shake his hand ask if there's been any trouble.

"No. Luis said Chavez understood having to get the cattle to grass and didn't really seem to care one way or the other. The vaqueros and the cattle rode out of the canyon peaceful as can be. Chavez is expecting them back Monday. He did tell Luis that his business in town would be finished by then and when they got back it would be time to start building the new ranch."

As pleased as I am that the vaqueros were able to leave the canyon with the cattle and without trouble, it isn't comforting knowing that I am the "business" that Chavez,

Diego and the others planned to take care of. I can tell by Cisco's face that he's thinking the same thing.

I turn Horse around and ride the last mile with Cisco. Looking at Frank's property from a cattleman's perspective, it is easy to see that it is set up in a perfect area. There's a nice little, open box canyon just a half mile behind the house and a small stream that feeds the pond. Add in that there is plenty of good grass, and there's no reason for the cattle to look to go anywhere else. I don't know a lot about raising cattle, but it seems like there is room, water and grazing for quite a few more.

Luis, having seen the box canyon, rides up and says they'll move the cattle up there. It will be easy for two men, even one, to hold the cattle steady there until they grow used to their new home. Cisco and I leave the vaqueros to finish up, and we ride over to Frank's place.

It doesn't seem quite so eerie to walk inside with Cisco there, and we build a nice fire to take the edge off the cold, to make lunch and maybe to push the last odd feelings out the chimney. The place is small, but with one or two vaqueros staying at the canyon mouth and maybe another on the front porch, it will work until they add a couple rooms onto the cabin. Winter is gone, and while spring nights can still get chilly out here, no one is going to be in danger of freezing.

We just about have supper ready when four of the vaqueros ride up, leaving Roberto and Juan, who always seems to get left behind, to watch the cattle. We talk while we eat. When we finish, Benito rides back to the canyon, bringing supper for Roberto and Juan. The vaqueros are happy with the ranch and looking forward to meeting with Thurm and working out the details of buying it. They mention again that they don't have much money, but I tell them it won't be a problem and the town would be happy to work something out to have six new residents of Dry Springs.

When I am ready to leave, Cisco walks out with me, again asking if he can come with me tomorrow morning. I already knew he wanted to, especially after watching Frank die and having to help kill the men who did it. But I tell him no.

"Cisco, our weddings are Sunday. Maria has been through too much this year, and it isn't right that she should have to worry—again. You stay with the men tonight. Help them settle in. Tell them about the town. Tomorrow, bring two of them in, introduce them around town and help them get set up with supplies. Ray will give them credit until they can sell some cattle, and you can introduce them to Thurm."

He looks at me, not happy or in agreement. "You are getting married too."

"That is true. But there are differences—the most important being that they are coming for me, not you. Plus, I am the sheriff. You can stay in town tomorrow and help Clybs, if he needs it. But, Maria has already lost one husband, and I won't let her lose another one."

With that, I turn and ride away.

Nineteen - Maria

Cat had put Enyeto to bed and had fallen asleep beside him, and with Cisco out with the vaqueros, Maria was all alone, something she had come to fear. Brock had stopped by to let her know that everything had gone well, the men were set up safely on Frank's ranch, Chavez suspected nothing and it would all be over tomorrow.

But still, Maria was scared.

She loved Cisco and looked forward to the wedding Sunday. But it had been a very tough year. One morning, not so long ago, she had woken up in her small home on Chavez's Rancho del Cielo in Tesuque, with a husband, a home and a baby growing inside her, so new P'oe didn't even know. Within a week, all of that was gone, along with almost everything and everyone she knew. P'oe was murdered in Coyote Creek. Chavez stole virtually everything she owned, and she lost the baby as they escaped Chavez and the Apaches. If it wasn't for Brock, and later the Muache Indians, she was certain that she, along with Cisco, Enyeto and Cat, wouldn't have survived the trip from her former home in Tesuque to Dry Springs.

She had moved on, as women were required to do living out here, but she had not forgotten the pain, or the sense of loss, or the realization of how quickly everything can be taken away.

She was grateful for Cat, and of course for Enyeto, as well as for her new friends and her new life in Dry Springs. Cisco was a good man, and she had always loved him. Secretly, she knew if Cisco had asked for her hand before P'oe, she would have married him. She had always loved both men, and still did. Maria understood that as bad as things had been, they could certainly be much worse, and not a day went by that she didn't thank God for what she had. But, not a day went by that she didn't ask God why the things that happened to her did. God had yet to answer.

And so, just when she was starting to feel safe again, when the pain of the losses had almost become bearable, Frank was killed and Cisco, along with Brock and Huck, nearly so. Maria was a strong woman, but she doubted that she could survive losing Cisco. She never said anything to him, but she hated it when he went away. Sometimes, when he was gone, she was so scared for him, for her, she found it hard to breath. This last trip, when Frank was killed, made all those feelings seem very real and very realistic.

And now, three days before their wedding, Cisco was gone again, this time riding toward hired killers. Cisco was a good man, and he had been working with Brock for the last couple of months, learning to shoot, but Maria knew he was no match for hired killers. Cisco knew that too, but there would have been no way to stop him from helping his friends, especially Brock. Maria knew Cisco was at the ranch and not going to the canyon in the morning. She knew that other men were helping, and she knew it must be even worse for Sophie, since Brock was the man they were trying to kill. She even knew that if the very worst happened and she lost Cisco, she would have a job, a place to live and friends. But she was still scared, more scared than she had been in Coyote Creek, in the back of the wagon when she had lost the baby and didn't know if she would get through the day.

And so, for now, she sat in the dark with a glass of bourbon and her thoughts. She prayed for Cisco. She prayed for Brock. She prayed for all the men of Dry Springs. And for the first time in her life, she prayed for someone to die. She prayed that Chavez, and the other men waiting in Coyote

Canyon, would die quickly and without inflicting any more pain, any more death. She knew this was wrong in the eyes of God, and if things happened as she prayed, she would ask for God's forgiveness and pay the price for the sin of wishing death on others. But it was a price she was willing to pay.

Maria pulled the blanket tighter against the cold, which came as much from inside of her as it did outside. She took the last sip of bourbon and fell into a troubled sleep as the fire slowly died.

Twenty – Brock

I'm leaving the house before Sophie is up, but I feel much better having talked to her last night. We've always been able to talk, at least since the first time I saw her and couldn't get a word out, but last night was different. I don't know if I had any doubts about how she felt about me, or Huck, or us, but I certainly don't now. I also know she's ready to welcome Dusty as a part of our family, and after our talk last night, so am I. She also made it abundantly clear that she expects me—all of us—to come home safely today and to have ended this threat once and for all.

And with that—and a clear head for the first time since Frank was killed—Horse and I head to town. My first stop is the church to meet up with Matt. He wanted one last time to pray in his new church before we set out this morning. I figure anything that helps us come to peace with what we're riding out to do is a good thing. Mine was a conversation with Sophie; his is with God. I'm guessing he's already talked to Stacy.

He steps out, says good morning and starts to strap on his gun. I notice immediately that he does it in a way that lets me know he's done this often and that he hasn't always been a reverend. It's clear I don't know much about Matt's pre-Dry Springs life, and I make a note to ask him about it, just not today.

"Morning, Rev. Make your peace?"

Matt smiles. "I did that a long time ago, Brock. Just went in this morning to let him know what we're up to."

I smile back. "I was thinking about one of your sermons, Rev. If I got it right, it was, 'Vengeance is mine, I will repay, says the Lord.' How's that work with you ridin' out with us this morning?"

Smiling, Matt looks at me, "Glad to see you're paying attention on Sundays. Always kinda figured you were there because Sophie was making you come. And Romans 12:19, that's one of my favorites. Even though I am a man of God, I still struggle with some of the things I read, and so, on this one, I figure we'll help the Lord out, just a little bit."

We walk our horses down the middle of the completely empty street, toward the Dusty Rose and Hattie's. Just as we arrive, Will comes walking out of the Dusty Rose, pistol holstered and his shotgun slung over his left shoulder.

"I'll need to pick up my horse down at the livery. Is Dusty riding with us?"

Just then, Dusty steps out of Hattie's and quietly answers for himself. "Yes."

I'm facing the three of them, looking away from the direction we just came from.

Dusty says, "I talked Nolan into making us a little breakfast before we go. Should be ready 'bout now."

Feeling anxious to get going, I say, "Maybe it'd be best if we skip breakfast and start riding. No idea how long this is gonna take."

Dusty looks at Matt and Will, then back at me. "I don't think Chavez and his men are expecting us, so an extra half hour or so shouldn't make too much difference. Plus,"—he looks directly at me—"it'll give you time to deputize me."

And then, looking past me, he adds, "And maybe it'll give me a chance to get to know my grandson a little bit."

"I'll deputize you, said I would, and I guess I wouldn't mind a little breakfast if everyone wants a bite. But Huck's had enough surprises in the past few months, and I don't need him any more confused about today than he already is. We're not going back to the house and waking him."

"You don't have to." I turn around, and there he is, standing with Ray.

Ray looks at Huck and then me. "He was coming whether I wanted him to or not, so I figured I'd walk down with him." He walks right past me and offers his hand to Dusty, who quickly accepts it. "My name's Ray Hinton. I'm Sophie's father, Huck's grandfather and pleased to meet you. This young man"—he looks back and waves Huck over—"is your grandson, Huck."

As I stand there, wondering once again how I lost control of the situation, Matt speaks up. "Seems like breakfast is a good idea. Hope Nolan's got enough for all of us."

The others start to walk up the steps to Hattie's, and I follow behind. As soon as we're seated, Nolan starts to bring out enough food to feed ten men. Huck sits between Ray and Dusty, and they are soon lost in conversation, the three of them talking as if there is no one else at the table and as if they've known each other for years. Matt and Will pretend to be fascinated with their food, not saying a word, and I just watch and listen.

Ray talks for a bit about how he and Ellen founded Dry Springs and the changes it's been through over the past twenty years. I'm surprised as Huck readily tells how his dad was killed and what it was like the day of the gunfight with Kurt and his men. He tells his favorite story, how he killed a bear, but doesn't say anything about the night Frank was killed. He talks about what a great mom Sophie is and looks at me briefly as he talks about all the things we do together. And last, Dusty tells a few stories of life on the trail, enough to make a young teenage boy ready to saddle up and ride out today in search of his own adventures and his own stories.

A half hour has turned into an hour when I finally point out that we have to leave. We all thank Nolan, who refuses payment for breakfast, and walk back to the livery to pick up Will's and Dusty's horses. Ray and Huck shake Dusty's hand, and I hear Ray invite him for dinner tonight, saying that Sophie's looking forward to meeting him. Huck runs over, gives me a hug, and without another word, is gone. Ray smiles as he reminds me I promised to marry his daughter Sunday and that he's already paid for the food and would hate to see it go to waste. He wishes us good luck and turns to catch up with Huck, and the four of us are left alone.

I go through the formality of deputizing Dusty, wondering to myself if it might not be easier to just deputize the whole town. A couple of people are starting to move around in front of their shops, and so, not wanting any additional delays, we start riding.

After a few minutes of quiet, I remind everyone, looking directly at Dusty, that we're going out there to arrest these men, not to kill them.

Dusty lets that settle in for a couple of minutes and then starts. "Brock, I know that's what you want to do and that you hope it might actually happen. But I've spent quite a bit more time with Chavez, and others like him, than you have, and I'm telling you now, he's not coming in peacefully."

He looks around at each of us and then at our weapons. "When you're done asking them to give themselves up—and they're done laughing—everyone here better be ready to use these guns, and if you're not, it'd be best to turn around now."

Will speaks up first. "He's right, Brock, and you know it. I'll buy drinks for the house for a week if we're riding back in a couple of hours with the four of them tied up nice and neat on their horses and the biggest problem we're facing is figuring out how to get a circuit judge to come to Dry Springs."

I look at the reverend. "Matt?"

"Just like you, I know what I signed up for. The Lord has tried to teach me to see the best in all men, but like I told you earlier, I still struggle with some of the teachings. I don't see a way this ends without shooting. I've got words I'll say when we're done, but I hope to be praying over the four of them and none of us, and I'll do what I have to do to see that that's the way it goes."

In a day, a week, a year, full of surprises, here comes another one. I turn to a man I only met two days ago, know hardly at all and ask for what I guess could be called fatherly advice.

"Dusty, you say you know Chavez and men like him. When we get there, what do you suggest we do?"

"Matt, I see you've got a rifle, but, Will, you've just got the shotgun?"

"Yep. Works well for up-close work. Haven't owned a rifle since the war."

"Switch that shotgun out for Brock's rifle." We make the switch.

"They don't know we're coming, and when we get there, they won't know how many we are. Brock's already stood up to them once, alone, so once they get over the initial surprise of him being there at all, they won't be surprised if we let them believe Brock's alone.

"We'll ride until we get about a half mile from the mouth of the canyon. We'll tie off the horses and walk the last bit. We'll stay quiet and out of sight until we know where they are. According to the vaqueros, there are four of them, so we'll want to account for all four before doing anything."

No one says anything, and we all keep listening.

"Once we know where they are, and I expect them to be overconfident and all together, we'll split up, with the three of us taking positions where we can use our rifles. Brock, once we're in place, you'll stay hidden and share your idea about the surrendering. If they like that idea and walk out with their hands up, we'll tie 'em up, throw 'em on their horses, and bring 'em back to your jail. Will, if that does happen, I'll split the cost of the drinks with you for the next week."

There's a little nervous laughter from everyone, and then Matt asks, "And if they don't?"

"We wait until they take the first shot at Brock, which they will, and then we start shooting—and we keep shooting until the four of them are dead."

This time there's no laughter, but no disagreement either. We are quickly at a good point to tie off the horses, even Horse, and we all take a minute to double-check our weapons and make sure they're loaded, no empty chambers. We start walking toward the canyon, sticking to the trees in case they happen to have a guard stationed up front.

The walk is uneventful, but I can feel the tension grow with each step. The day's rest seems to have done Dusty some good, because he looks better than he did when he left the house Wednesday night. After just a few minutes in the canyon we hear voices. It doesn't take long to hear four different voices, and it's clear they have no idea we're here.

There's not much left to say, so Matt starts working his way up the left side of the canyon, and Will and Dusty take the right side. I give them a few minutes to find good spots and settle in, and then I start forward. I've spent quite a bit of time on the trail by myself, but I have rarely felt so all alone. It's good having friends with me, and I know they're out there, but I have zero confidence that Chavez and his men are going to surrender, which means what I am really doing is offering myself as bait—exchanging a doomed demand for surrender for information on exactly where they are hidden.

I come to the very edge of a small clearing. On the other side, maybe seventy-five feet away, is a group of rocks and trees that offers them excellent coverage. I back up a couple of feet, find the biggest, thickest tree I can, check my gun one more time and yell, "Chavez, it's me, Brock, Sheriff Clemons. You and your men are under arrest."

Twenty-One - Brock

I had anticipated silence, angry denial or maybe gunshots, but what I didn't anticipate was Dusty being right and Chavez's response to be laughter.

"Good morning, Clemons. Me and my men were just trying to figure out the best way to draw you out of that tiny little town of yours, and you decide to just ride right up into our little canyon. I should thank you, but with all the trouble you've caused me over the last few months, I don't think I will."

"Chavez, I didn't ride out here to make things easier for you, but to arrest you. So, I'll ask you again to step out and allow me to do so. As for the other men you have with you, I have no reason that I know of to arrest them, but I also have no reason to trust them, so I'll ask them to step out as well, with all of you dropping your weapons. Once I've gathered up the weapons and have you tied up and ready to ride, you and I will head to town. I'll drop the weapons about a mile from here, right in the middle of the trail, and you other men can pick them up, along with your horses, on your way to somewhere else."

I'm not surprised, but Chavez doesn't agree to my terms. However, at least I tried and whatever happens from here on out is on him. It doesn't take long for him to share his plans for this morning.

"Sheriff, I do plan on riding into town today, but when I do, you'll be dead and I'll be ready to take over. I read the articles about you and this town, and without you, when those people see me, Diego and the others ride in, Dry Springs will be ours before nightfall. As a matter of fact, I think Diego here would like to be sheriff." I hear Diego laugh.

"The people of Dry Springs are different than they were and different than you expect. They don't need me to defend our town, and you'll find that out should you ever get a chance to ride in. However, I don't think it's going to be as easy as you think for you to ride out of here, at least if you plan on going upright. You've already tried to kill me once, and that didn't work out as you hoped."

"So, Miguel and the others did find you. When they didn't return, I wondered what happened to them."

Remembering that night in the forest, I clear up any remaining curiosity he might have. "They won't ever be returning."

"It is unfortunate that they were killed, but I have many vaqueros."

I'm giving up more information than I should, but I'm starting to get angry. "You have six less than you think you do, Chavez."

It doesn't take him long to figure out what I meant.

"I never should have let them go into town until after we killed you. Now, when we're done here, I will have to find those vaqueros and kill them too. Then, I will hire cowboys from my new town to work my ranch."

"If you do make it past me, you'll find your vaqueros a little south of here, but they'll be seven, not six. Cisco— you remember him—is with them and not happy at all that I wouldn't let him come with me this morning. It was Cisco and me who killed Miguel and the others, and after that night, plus what you did to him and his family, he has been looking forward to seeing you again."

As I talk, I'm starting to run out of patience.

"Chavez, you talk about killing as if it's easy. It isn't. But I don't think you know that. I know you have Diego and a couple of others with you. And you hide behind them like you do those rocks, like all cowards do. When I think of you, I think of a man who, on his own ranch, when he still had a ranch, even when surrounded by all his hired guns— including you, Diego—backed down to one man, me. And now, I watch as the four of you hide away in the hills like scared coyote pups, talking big, but with nothing left but talk, not even the cattle you stole."

Apparently, Chavez and the others have run out of patience too, because the conversation abruptly ends and gunfire begins.

It's hard to tell, but I'm guessing all four of them are firing at me, or at least at the tree. Until the others start to draw off some fire, I'm not poking my head out there. Fortunately, the boys don't wait long before they open up. I can hear rifle shots from the side Dusty and Will set up at, but nothing from Matt. The bullets coming my way slow down as at least two of the four turn their attention to Dusty and Will. This allows me to poke my head out—I'm down at ground level—in time to see Matt, about a hundred feet up the hill on my left side, stand up unseen, take careful aim, and with two quick shots from his rifle, take them from four men to three.

Matt immediately draws Diego's fire, and it turns out he's good, as he hits Matt in the leg as he's moving from a tree to a rock.

Will sees it too and yells up to Matt. "You OK?"

"Yeah. Got me in the leg, but the rifle and the trigger finger still work." The three surviving men put some rocks between them and Matt, so there's not much Matt can do, unless we flush them out. Chavez keeps firing at me, but Diego joins the third man as they pour fire at Will and Dusty. I keep Chavez pinned, but he's doing the same to me, and unless one of us gets lucky, we're at a stalemate.

The shooting between Will and Dusty and Diego and the other man is furious. It seems nonstop, but they have to be reloading. Unless someone runs out of ammunition, I don't see how this is going to end. I'm looking for ways to move to one side or another, but I can't do it without exposing myself to a clean shot from Chavez. I told him killing wasn't easy, and I don't see any reason to make it any easier. I keep firing, but more for effect now, and I've slowed down, conserving the bullets I have left. I'm focused more on Diego than Chavez and am frustrated that I can't help. As I'm getting close to taking a chance and shifting position, I hear a short scream from either Dusty or Will and then for a moment, no firing. When it starts up again, there is only one rifle firing from our side.

Diego yells out toward whoever is left.

"Looks like we got one. Come out now and we won't have to kill you too."

"I think I'll stay right here and keep fighting." It's Will. That means Dusty's been hit, and it's serious, or he'd still be firing. I can only hope he's not dead.

I watch as Will starts to work his way forward and left, hoping for a better angle and a clean shot. But in doing so, he exposes himself a little too much, and the third man, with a good shot, puts a bullet through Will's shoulder. Will drops to the ground, desperately trying to reach his fallen rifle, and the third man, forgetting Will's not alone, stands up to finish him off. He never gets the shot off, as I drop him with a shot to the head.

I fear Dusty's dead. Will's out of the fight and bleeding quite a bit, and Matt is down, though maybe not hurt too bad. Two of their men are down, but Chavez and Diego are both unhurt and unwilling to give up.

Out of the corner of my eye, I see Matt shift his position a little, enough to get off a shot at the spot Diego was in before he moved over and started in on Dusty and Will. With both of them down, it makes sense he'll be back. I don't have to wait long. I start firing at Chavez, and I can see a little movement from behind their rocks. And just as Diego's hat comes into view, Matt takes the shot. Another short yell, and the hat fades from view.

Chavez turns and opens up on Matt, who manages to get back behind cover. Chavez shifts to where he can't be seen by Matt, but can keep firing at me. After a minute, he stops, and so do I, unable to do much more than hope for a ricochet anyway. I'm wondering what we're going to do next, when Chavez yells from behind the rocks.

"Well, Clemons, it's just me and you. All my men are dead, and yours are either dead or out of the fight. Tell you what. I'll drop my rifle, holster my pistol and walk out, and we can settle this once and for all."

I don't move. "Don't you think enough men have died here already?"

"No. I can stay here all day, while your men bleed to death. Or, we do this my way, and after I kill you, I won't kill your men. I'll make it easy on you. I'm coming out, gun holstered. You can shoot me from behind that tree, but if you do, I don't think you could live with yourself."

Hand at his side, but empty, Chavez comes out from the protective rocks, on the side where Matt can't reach him. Knowing he's right about the men bleeding and that I can't shoot him this way, I step out, gun holstered.

"Why?"

"Your dad took my money, and after what you did with Hinojosa and the others, even my own men didn't respect me. I figured the best way to get back at you was to kill both of you. Always thought it was funny that sick old man never wanted to meet you. Pit he's dead. I wanted to kill him myself. When I'm done here, I'll take over your little town. Won't be long before I'm rich again, and then I'll go back down to Santa Fe and make them all pay for what they did."

"You seem pretty sure you can beat me. If you surrender now, I'll take you back to Dry Springs, alive, and we'll have a trial."

"I like our chances here better than with a jury."

As I am processing the word "our," Diego comes out from the other side—quite alive and perfectly healthy.

Diego looks at Chavez and then me. "Your man up there shot Eduardo, who you'd already killed. He shoulda waited to see more than the hat before he fired. Did cost me a perfectly good hat, but I think it was worth it—don't you? I think I'll take yours when we're done here. Little bigger than I like, but it'll do."

"It won't fit you."

I glance to my right to see who said that, and it's Dusty—not dead, not wounded and walking out of the trees and taking up a spot on my right side, across from Diego.

"Look, Diego," Chavez says. "It's the sick old man, come out to make things easy on us. Nice trick, but you shoulda stayed down in Tucson, or where we thought you were dead, and maybe we'd have forgot about you. Now, Diego's got to kill you while I kill your boy."

As he's saying that, I see Diego go for his gun. We all do the same. Chavez and I draw and fire at the same time. He misses. I don't. I'm turning toward Diego before Chavez hits the ground, but it's already over. Diego was much faster than Dusty, and Dusty's falling, having been hit by Diego's first—and last—shot. But before Diego or I get off a second shot, Dusty, on his way down, drops Diego with a shot to the forehead.

I get to Dusty as his knees are giving out and help him gently to the ground. I see the blood spreading rapidly across his chest, and as I start to unbutton his coat, he reaches up and holds my arm.

"I didn't have long anyway." I can hear Will moaning, but I can't take my eyes off of Dusty's—off of my father's—eyes.

I have so much to say, so much I want to tell him, but I can't get a single word out as I watch him die. I grab his hand and hold it tightly and feel the sting of tears as they roll off of my face and onto his.

The bleeding, along with his breathing, starts to slow down, and with what must be a huge effort, he opens his eyes one last time, looks into mine and whispers, "I wish I had been a father to you."

I close his eyes and wipe mine, and then turn to check on Will.

Twenty-Two - Brock

As I'm running to where Will fell, I yell up to Matt.

"You still alive up there?"

His sense of humor intact, Matt yells back, "My leg's shot up pretty good, but I can still marry you Sunday. How are Dusty and Will?"

Not ready to think about Dusty, I focus on Will. "I'm checking."

He's weak and unconscious, but fortunately for him the bullet went straight through his shoulder and the wound is clean. Even more fortunately, or he'd be dead from loss of blood, the wound is also expertly bandaged, front and back.

It turns out the last thing Dusty did before he saved my life was save Will's.

I turn to go back to where I had been hiding, again yelling up to Matt. "Let me get Will some water, and then I'll come check on you."

Calling back down, Matt asks, "How's Dusty?"

Before I can answer, I hear a voice behind me. "I've got water here, and you men go up and bring Matt down."

I look and there's Cisco, along with four of the vaqueros: Luis, Vic, Benito and Roberto, with Jose, and once again, Juan, being left behind to watch the cattle. The vaqueros easily follow Matt's nonstop talking up the hill,

161

while Cisco and I get a little water into Will, who wakes up long enough to smile.

I cover Will with my coat and look at Cisco. "How…"

"I know why you didn't want me here, and you are a good friend. But when we heard the shots, I knew that for me to be a good friend too, I needed to be here. I should have been here from the beginning. I jumped on Regalo and took off, and without hesitation or a word, Luis and the others followed. I am only sorry we didn't get here sooner. If we had, maybe your father would be alive."

"Cisco, you are a good friend. I have none better. As for Dusty, I don't think he expected to ride back today. He was very sick. He was spitting up blood at the house Wednesday night. I didn't know him very well, but isn't it better to go out like he did, rather than rotting away in some bed?"

"Maybe, but I think he might have wanted to see his son get married."

Before I can respond, which is good since I don't know what to say, the vaqueros are back with Matt. They set him down next to Will, who seems to have improved a little with the water and the coat.

Cisco and I start to look at Matt's leg. Luis, looking at the wounded men, speaks up. "If you and Cisco can take care of these men for now, we will begin burying the dead."

I look up, I guess with a surprised look on my face, and Luis continues. "I know what they did and who they are. We bury them for us, and for God, not for them."

The thought of the men I've left unburied in the past year, by choice and necessity, comes into my head, but that will have to be looked at another time. I nod to Luis.

"I'll take my father back with us and bury him in town."

As Cisco and I start working on Matt's leg, the others start digging the graves. After a few minutes, during which we do what we can for Matt and Will, at least until we can get them back to Dry Springs and to Doc, Vic comes back and hands me an open leather bag with quite a bit of money inside.

"This was on Chavez's horse."

I look at Cisco, then back at Vic.

"Thank you. You and your men keep the horses, saddles and weapons. You'll need them to get started on your new ranch. As for the money, I'll take it with me. I'll use a little to pay Doc for the work he has to do, and then I'll use the rest to pay off the—your—ranch. Thurm will see that the money gets to Frank's family in Guatemala and that you receive the deed to the ranch. If there is any money left over, and if we're all in agreement, it will go to the church."

Matt and Cisco agree immediately, and I look at Vic, who seems surprised by all of this, including being asked his opinion.

"Of course."

With that settled, I look down at Matt and Will, then back at Cisco.

"We need to get these men back to town and to Doc right away. I'll go get our horses."

Vic stops me. "Please. Take our horses. We will bring yours to town later, when we are done here."

I hate to leave Horse, but she's a half mile away, and Will needs immediate help. I'm afraid that without Doc, Matt might lose his leg. I thank Vic, who helps Cisco and I tie Dusty onto one of the horses. Cisco climbs on Regalo, and we help Matt settle in behind him. Matt's in obvious pain but, for once, doesn't say a word. Vic gives me his horse, and then he and Benito gently help Will settle in in front of me.

The ride back takes about an hour, but it's a tough one. Will and Matt have both passed out, having lost a lot of blood, and the ride is not helping at all. I'm thankful again for Dusty, because whether Will makes it or not, he wouldn't even have a chance if Dusty hadn't patched him up.

Cisco and I aren't talking, and even Matt is uncharacteristically quiet, so I've got some time to think a little about my life. The advantage of leading a simple life is that most choices are easy to make, though not always easy to execute, and not a lot of thought is required. By design, I've tried to lead a simple life and, until a few months ago, a solitary one. But as I ride back to Dry Springs, back toward my soon-to-be wife, my new son, my job as sheriff and my friends, I realize my life is no longer solitary, or simple.

I'm holding onto Will so that he doesn't fall off the horse. He's close to death, shot while protecting me, and next to us is Cisco, doing the same with Matt. These men, none of whom I knew a year ago, are now dear friends, and one or more of them may not see tomorrow. And trailing behind us, dead, strapped over a horse, is my father, a man I pursued for more than two years, met two days ago, and watched die an hour ago.

Since the first day I rode into Dry Springs, my life has been filled with enemies and death. As hard as I try to find an answer, I don't know how I could have stopped any of it from happening, and I'm beginning to become concerned about how to stop it from happening again. Still, left with far more questions than answers, I look up to see Dry Springs in the distance.

As we get close to down, a rider comes racing out from behind the Dusty Rose. After a minute, I can see it's Huck. For once he listened to me and stayed where I asked him too, but it's obvious he's been sitting on Spirit for a while, waiting for us to return. He rides up and takes it all in in a single glance, including the fact that his grandfather, who he only met a few hours ago, is dead.

"Huck, I'm sorry about all of this, but you have to ride back to town faster than you rode out here and let Doc know we're coming in. Matt and Will are shot up pretty good, and they've both lost a lot of blood. After you tell Doc, go tell your grandpa Ray to meet us at Doc's. Let your mom know what you've seen here, and have her stop and get Stacy. She needs to tell her Matt's been shot, but he's going to live, and then they need to head straight to Doc's. Then go get Maria. Be sure the first thing you tell her is that Cisco's OK, but also tell her that we need her help."

With his head tucked into Spirit's neck, Huck turns and gallops back to town, straight to Doc's. Afraid of what it will do to Will and Matt if we travel any faster, Cisco and I continue at our slow pace, with each step seeming to take forever. By the time we get to Doc's, Huck is gone, but there are plenty of men waiting to help.

Ray and Nolan take Will from in front of me, and Shawn and Thurm help Matt off the back of Cisco's horse. Will doesn't wake, but Matt does, long enough to remind everyone that Sunday's service is at 10:00 and he expects them all to be there. That's probably the best sign we could have hoped for from Matt, and Doc even laughs a bit as they're carried in.

Maria, Stacy and Sophie arrive at the same time. Stacy doesn't slow down—she just races into Doc's place. Maria runs up to Cisco, and I'm expecting him to get a hug and maybe a kiss from the woman he's marrying Sunday. Suddenly, she is pounding his chest with her fists, screaming at him. "You promised! You promised!"

I look away from Cisco and Maria and turn to Sophie, forgetting to say I love you or even hello, and ask, "What's happening? What's wrong?"

Her answer seems obvious, but not too helpful. "She's upset."

"About what? He's OK."

"She's not!"

Still not understanding, I ask, "What do you mean?"

Sophie stops and shakes her head, looking down at the ground. When she looks up, she asks, "When you moved everyone from Tesuque to here, did you ever see Maria cry, or even get upset?"

"No."

"In that one week, she lost her husband, her baby and her home. You were attacked by Apaches, and she watched her brother-in-law Danny get killed. And you never saw her cry."

"I guess I never thought about it."

"Well, she has. It's been hard for her to think of anything else other than what happened to her, to her family, to her life, in that week. But, she moved here. And she's in love with Cisco and has her sister and little Enyeto. She's made friends and has a job. She's getting married Sunday! Remember? This is her fresh start, her chance to rebuild.

"And then, two weeks ago, you take Cisco hunting, and Frank is killed. She knows that could have just as easily been Cisco, just like I know it could have been you. Even worse for me, that it was supposed to be you. And that brought back all of the feelings she has tried so hard to bury. And last night, Cisco promised Maria that he wouldn't leave Frank's place, that he wouldn't ride to the canyon. She knew it was selfish, but she made him promise anyway. And when you rode up with Dusty strapped to a horse, as sad as we are for him, and for you, we were both relieved. But it could have been you. It could have been Cisco. And so now she's angry. Not just for today, but for Frank, and Danny, and P'oe, and her baby."

There are tears streaming down Sophie's face, and I begin to understand that it must be much harder on the people left behind to wait than it is on the people who are in the fight. The problem is I don't know what to do about it. Sophie, knowing this isn't the time for a conversation I now know we have to have, kisses me gently on the lips and pulls away. At the same time, Maria, seeming spent but somehow better, pulls away from Cisco, and both women follow Stacy into Doc's.

That leaves the men waiting out front, so I spend a few minutes telling them about what happened since we first walked into Coyote Canyon this morning. Some of it is new to Cisco too. Not knowing how long Doc and the girls will be working on Will and Matt, I make a couple of suggestions.

I ask Shawn and Huck to take the horses down to the livery. Before they do, Shawn takes me aside.

"Brock, I have a little experience with bodies and coffins, another horrible thing I learned in the war. Doc's gonna be busy for a while, so if you want, I'll take Dusty with me, build a coffin and get him ready."

I hadn't even thought of that. I'm so focused on Doc saving Matt's leg and Will's life that I forgot that I have to bury my father.

"I appreciate it, Shawn. Thank you."

Ray walks over to me and quietly says, "I'll go down too. I'm sure Shawn can use some help, and I want to be sure Huck is OK. Sad thing is, I spent a good part of the day thinking about how much I enjoyed Dusty's stories at breakfast this morning. I was looking forward to dinner tonight, and maybe a few after that. I'm sorry about what happened, Brock."

I thank him, and then the three of them start walking down to the livery, Ray taking the horse with Dusty.

At some point since we'd been back to town, I must have grabbed Chavez's bag, or maybe I carried it the whole way back from the canyon. But here it is, in my left hand. I walk over to Thurm and explain that after he pays Doc and now Shawn, I want him to pay off Frank's ranch and send the money to his family. And I tell him if there's any money left to add it to the church fund. Thurm smiles his agreement, takes the bag and heads over to the bank.

That leaves me, Cisco and Nolan. Since there isn't much we can do, I suggest to Nolan that he head back to Hattie's and help Nerissa. When he hesitates, I tell him we can call him back right away if anyone needs anything.

I loosen up my gun and take a seat on Doc's second step. Cisco takes the chair Doc keeps on the front porch. It's getting to be late in the afternoon, and the spring air is more a reminder of winter than a predictor of summer. I button my coat, and Cisco does the same. A few people are on the street, but no one comes over and says anything, somehow seeming to know we need a little time.

Maria, looking like she feels much better, pokes her head out Doc's front door.

"Doc says Matt's gonna keep his leg, but he took two bullets, including one to the knee, and he's probably going to have a permanent limp to remind him of today. He hasn't stopped talking since Stacy got here, and now he's telling her what kind of cane he wants. Doc told him to shut up and save his strength, and Stacy says if he doesn't listen to Doc, she'll find a cane and use it to shut him up." She smiles. "Matt's gonna be fine."

I smile back, relieved that a limp is the worst of it for Matt. I'm sure there's a sermon in there somewhere, and we'll all be listening to it sometime in the next few weeks.

Cisco asks, "And Will?"

"Doc doesn't know. The wound's clean, and he said that without the bandages, Will would have bled out. He's trying to get some water in him and says we'll know more in the next few hours. Sophie's helping Doc change the bandages while Stacy tries to settle Matt down."

Maria steps outside and walks over to Cisco. Cisco stands up, takes her hand and looks at me, as Huck walks back from the livery.

"I finished up the horses, and grandpa sent me back down—said you could use the company."

Cisco, needing time with Maria as much as I need to be with Huck, starts to walk down the steps. "You and Huck yell if you need anything?"

I nod a yes, and they walk past us and start heading to the store. But it's clear they just need some time to talk and digest what's happened. And then, it's just me and Huck. He takes a seat next to me, and I drape my arm around his shoulder.

"Since the first day I met you, bad people have come into our lives and bad things have happened. Kurt, the Apaches and now Chavez. We've had friends killed, friends who died way too young and for no good reason. I wish I could tell you why, to make sense of it for you, but I can't make sense of it for me. I keep thinking about what I could have done differently, how I could have stopped any of this before the killing started. Should I have seen it coming? But I can't see it different than how it happened. Huck, I just don't know what I coulda done. I'm gonna keep thinking 'bout what's happened, but I can't see the answers."

"But, Huck, I promise you this: that's the end of it. It started last year with Kurt, and then when I found Cisco under attack from the robbers. Everything since then has been related to that and Chavez, including Frank's murder. But they're all dead now. There's no one else."

"Is Mom going to be OK? She and Maria were at the house, and they were both crying all morning. She said there was nothing I could do to help, 'cept stay close to the house."

In thinking about what Huck said, things are starting to become a little more clear. One thing is certain—it is going to be much harder to be married than it was traveling by myself. It will be worth it, but I have much more to learn than I thought.

"They were just upset because they were afraid something was going to happen to us."

"What about Will?"

"I don't know son. Doc's good at what he does, and Mom's helping, so all we can is pray."

"And Dusty?"

"I wish I could have gotten to know him. I wish you could have. He was already dying. He had tuberculosis, so I don't think he had very long, but even if it had just been for a little while…"

I look up and see Ray walking back down the street.

"Shawn's getting started on the coffin. We got Dusty all cleaned up. Gave him a new shirt—the bullet holes ruined the first one."

Wanting to make sure I heard right, I ask, "Bullet holes?"

"Yes. One in the chest, and one in the stomach."

That means when he walked out and stood with me, and even when he patched Will up, he'd already been gut shot.

"Ray, was the gut shot bandaged?"

"No, why?"

"I thought he had faked getting shot so he could back me up if needed. And I did need it. But at the end, we each only fired one shot, which means he'd already been shot when he helped Will and when he stood with me. He could have bandaged himself and maybe saved himself, but he didn't."

Twenty-Three - Brock

The crowd slowly and somberly worked its way to the front of the Dry Springs Church of the Resurrection. Like everyone else in town, Matt thought his beautiful new church would open for the first time tomorrow, with a sermon he'd been working on for weeks and not one, but two weddings. He also hadn't planned on being shot the day before and knowing he could only stand with help and for a couple of minutes. He kept his seat, watching as everyone settled in, hating that he wasn't at the front door to greet them. He also found it just a little odd that before giving his first talk in the new church, he had to take a couple shots of whiskey, even if it was to dull the pain in his leg. It hadn't done much, and Doc was probably right that he shouldn't be up, but unless it had been his own funeral, he wasn't going to miss this.

As the last couple of people walked in, Matt asked Cisco and Nolan to help him to the pulpit, which he leaned against, gripping the sides tightly with both hands as he looked out over the church, Stacy at his side. Cisco and Nolan stayed with him, slightly behind, but ready, Matt knew, to catch him if he started to fall.

"Good morning, and welcome to the first service at the Church of the Resurrection. Our church. Your church. Tomorrow, I'll talk about how this church was built and thank all of the good people who helped to make this possible. But not today.

"As a matter of fact, in what is probably a surprise to many of you, I'd like to start with a moment of silence. As most of you know, our own Will is over at Doc's fighting for his life, having been shot yesterday in defense of this town and his friends. So, as you sit in the pews that Will built, let's take a moment and pray for him."

A full minute passed, which Matt knew is a long time for a group to stay silent, but he wanted everyone to really think about Will.

"At first, I was a little sad that our first time together here in our church would be for a funeral, but the more I thought about it, the more I thought it was appropriate.

"The weddings tomorrow are going to be great. We have all been looking forward to them for a while now, and we still should be. Four of my favorite people are getting married, and I couldn't be happier for them or prouder that I get to perform the ceremonies. But the truth is, the weddings could be held anywhere and they would still be joyous occasions. Two people, or in this case four, committing themselves to a lifetime together is one of the greatest gifts we can give each other—no matter where we do it. Don't get me wrong, it's better in the Church, but you understand what I'm saying."

A little tension relieving laughter rippled through the crowd.

"But a funeral? Those are for churches. A man dies, he needs to be sent off right. He needs his friends and family around him, and he needs the strength, the power and the glory of a church to mark the day, to remember the life he lived here and send him on his greatest journey, to his new life. And today, that's what we're doing.

"Having said that, it might strike some of us as odd that we are here today to celebrate the life of a man none of us knew."

Matt looked down at Brock, who was sitting in the first row with Sophie, Huck and Ray.

"But, maybe, in a way, we all knew him.

"I don't know if he was a good man. He was a trapper and a ranch hand when he could be and a gambler when he couldn't. He was Brock's father for more than twenty years when he didn't want to be and for three days when he did.

"I know he saved my life. He saved Will's life. And he saved his son Brock's life. And he gave up whatever time he had left so that he could. Seems like the act of a good man to me.

"Before we rode out yesterday to Coyote Canyon, we had breakfast at Hattie's. Thank you, Nolan and Nerissa, for opening early. It was Dusty who asked that we have breakfast, that we sit together and talk before leaving for something that we all knew some of us might not come back from. Ray and Huck joined us, and Huck, even if only for an hour, got to meet and spend time with his grandfather. I watched as Ray, Huck and Dusty talked and laughed throughout the time they had together.

"Ray said that Dusty told some great stories, and if even half of them were true, he had led a fascinating life. Brock said he sat up with Dusty, his father, most of Wednesday night and learned enough to forgive him for what he'd done—or not done. If it's good enough for Brock, it works for me—and I hope, for you too.

"Ray asked that Dusty be buried on the same knoll with his beloved wife, Ellen. Said it's the family plot, and even if it was only for a couple of days, Dusty was family. I know some of you would want to help, but Brock said the family would like to bury him in private, maybe say a few words of their own.

"I did ask Brock if he wanted to say anything here this morning, but he's not ready. So, I ask God to take this man softly and quickly to what we all hope is a better place. I ask you to keep Dusty and his family in your prayers. We've lost too many good men in this town the past few months, and I'm not ready to lose another friend, so I'm asking you to also join me and keep Will in your prayers too.

"And last, please stand and join me in Psalm 23, which I find to be the most comforting passage in the Bible and never more appropriate than it is this morning."

Everyone rose, and as their voices rang out, sounding beautiful on this first day of the Dry Springs Church of the Resurrection, Matt, who was weakening quickly, held onto the pulpit and listened, eyes closed and heart open, certain that Dusty and God could hear them.

The Lord is my Shepherd; I shall not want.

He maketh me to lie down in green pastures: he leadeth me beside the still waters.

He restoreth my soul; he leadeth me in the paths of righteousness for his name's sake.

Yea, though I walk through the valley of the shadow of death, I will fear no evil; for thou art with me; thy rod and thy staff they comfort me.

Thou preparest a table before me in the presence of mine enemies: thou anointest my head with oil; my cup runneth over.

Surely goodness and mercy shall follow me all of my life: and I will dwell in the house of the Lord for ever.

Twenty-Four - Brock

Standing in front of that church, in front of all our family and friends, was in some ways scarier than standing in front of Kurt, or Chavez. At least then, I felt I had some sort of control of what was going to happen. Today, I felt as if I was being swept away, almost as if I was watching myself from above. In a day full of surprises, one of them was that Thurm had secretly purchased an organ and had it delivered and set up in the church. Another, and larger, surprise was that Thurm can play the organ and played the "Wedding March" as Sophie walked in.

It was only a few months ago, my first day in Dry Springs, when Ray invited me to his home for dinner and, as I started to walk up the steps to his porch, this woman, Sophie, turned and looked at me. I was literally dumbstruck by her beauty, and if Ray, and then Huck, hadn't covered for my sudden inability to speak, I don't know what I would have done. Her beauty was beyond anything I had ever seen, and I never imagined having the feeling again that I had when I first saw her. I was wrong.

As she started to walk down that aisle, her arm wrapped around her proud father's, I was stunned into silence again. The dress that Maria made was perfect, as was everything about Sophie. Someday I'll tell her that I barely heard a word of the ceremony, as all I could think about was whether I'd be able to speak. It was fortunate for me that Matt, not surprisingly, had plenty to say, because it gave me time to begin to recover. I'll tell Sophie someday how I wasn't sure I'd be able to talk at all until I heard her speak first and how, suddenly, it was the easiest thing in the world for me to say, "I do."

The rest of the day seemed to race by, but in the best way possible. It was long and spectacular, but now, finally, it is just the two of us. Ken James was nice enough to ask Huck to stay at their place with Tom for the night, and Ray pretended that he'd had too much to drink and would be better off staying at the Soft Beds until morning. Even Cat had taken Enyeto to stay with Nolan and Nerissa so Cisco and Maria could have some time to themselves.

Looking across the table at Sophie—who's still wearing her wedding dress, though now she's added a thick blanket to ward off the night chill—it is hard to imagine a more beautiful bride. I'm not sure when I'll ever wear this suit again, but since Sophie surprised me with it this morning, after having had it shipped all the way from London, and she seems to like it on me, I guess I'll be keeping it and wear it when she wants me to.

Of all the places I've been in my life, and even the places I've only dreamed of, I can't think of anywhere I would rather be than sitting on the front porch of Ray's home with Sophie. I know there's no one in the world I'd rather be with. I should be paying more attention as Sophie talks again about our first dance and what it felt like when she heard me say "I do," but I can't help but drift back to when we first met and everything we've been through together since that day. And now, looking across the table at the beautiful face I plan on seeing every day for the rest of my life, I'm still having trouble believing she said yes.

I relight my cigar for the third time, as I keep letting it go out while I'm lost in my thoughts and Sophie's beauty. I drift back into the conversation as Sophie is talking about Will.

"... and when they brought him into the church on the board, with Doc telling us Will insisted on coming, saying he could just as easily lie around in a church as he could in Doc's office ..."

I laugh easily at the thought of one of our wedding guests being carried in and laid across the top of two pews, which he had built, but just as much from the relief that Will was going to live. On a day filled with great news and a lifetime of memories, none was better than knowing my friend had survived and would make a full recovery if, as Doc said, "He lives through this wedding."

So much of the day is a blur, which I hope comes into focus with a little bit of time. Matt's sermon was beautiful, though I have no idea how he kept standing for so long, since, like Will, he should have been in bed. Everyone in town attended, and with the number of people who were there, I doubt there was anyone left on a ranch or farm for miles around. All the vaqueros came—even Juan wasn't left behind—their cattle just had to fend for themselves for a day.

Sophie was not the only beautiful bride today, as Maria looked stunning in her dress too. And from the look on her face all day, Cisco had been forgiven for riding out to Coyote Canyon. But, as I think about her pounding on his chest Friday, I hope my friend is very careful about the promises he makes to Maria and under only the direst of circumstances considers breaking one again.

I watch as Sophie pats her stomach. "... and I ate more and danced more than I ever have in one day. When did Nolan and Nerissa have time to make that much food?"

Though I don't remember eating at all, the amount and variety of food was as lavish as anything I'd ever seen.

And, as if Nolan and Nerissa had not prepared enough to feed the town for a week, including extra pies for the McClaskeys, it seemed that all of our guests treated the day as a pot-luck and brought something to share. Even the vaqueros rode in early, driving a lone cow before them, and by the time the wedding ceremony was over and the reception started, they had a barbecue going that lasted well into the night.

I take Sophie's hand. "I have been so focused on Chavez that I really didn't notice how hard everyone was working to make today perfect, which it was. And even when Friday was over, I spent most of yesterday with the funeral and worried about Will and Matt."

She squeezes my hand. "I am sorry I didn't get to meet your father." Suddenly, she jumps up and walks quickly into the house. She's back in a minute with an envelope, which she hands to me.

"I almost forgot. Ansel gave this to me after the reception. Said he found it on the dresser in Dusty's room when he was cleaning it out yesterday. Said it was leaning against the water pitcher and addressed to you."

I look down at a plain white envelope with my name written across the front, and for the first time today, I'm not smiling.

"Sophie, I don't know how I feel about Dusty, about my father. Is he the man who abandoned my mother and me twenty years ago, or the man who hid from me for the past two years, or the man who traded his life for mine? Or all of those? I figured this was one of those things I'd put away in a box and think about later, or maybe never, but now I'm thinking maybe that's one of the reasons people get married, to talk about things like this. I don't know."

I look up as she's sliding the envelope out of my hand. It's not sealed, and she gently pulls the letter out and holds it, her eyes asking if I want her to read it.

"Please."

She unfolds the paper and starts to read.

Brock,

I guess I didn't make it. I'm writing this after our breakfast, and I'd have torn it up if I came back from that canyon. The good news is that you're reading this, so you made it back.

There's so much I want to tell you, and now I won't be able to. They're not the kind of things that can be put into a letter, but should be shared over campfires, over meals, over time. I didn't know that until this week. And now, even if I live through tomorrow, I have so little time left.

I'm not going to offer you any excuses for my behavior; there aren't any. I'm glad we had even a little while to talk, and I hope it helps you understand. I'm also not going to offer you any advice. I don't feel I've earned the right to do that. But I will tell you, and it's my job to know people, you are a good man. Your mother did a good job of raising you. I wish I had met Sophie, but I did hear her that night in the saloon, and she is a strong woman. She reminds me of your mother.

I have a favor to ask of you, Brock. Though I've no right to ask, I have no one else.

Down in Tucson, there is an orphanage, St. Joseph's. There is an 8-year-old girl living there. Her name is Annabelle.

She is your sister.

Her mother died in childbirth, and she doesn't know who I am, though I see her a couple of times every year when I visit the orphanage. Whatever money I manage to get, I give to St. Joseph's, and they take good care of her.

I didn't realize until this week what a mistake I had made. She should have known me. I should have known her. Just like with you, I convinced myself she would be better off without me. What I was really thinking was that I would be better off without her and, I guess, without you. But I was wrong.

She is a beautiful little girl, and when I visited, I would watch her play for hours with the other kids. She seemed happy, or maybe that's what I needed to believe. I never held her. I never hugged her or gave her a kiss. When she was born, they took her away while I stayed with her mother and watched her die. It was almost two years before I saw Annabelle again. Miss Parsons, who runs the orphanage, said it would be better for her to not know who I was unless I planned on taking her, which I didn't. I should have.

Telling you this doesn't seem any more fair than everything else I've done, or not done, for you, but I wanted someone else to know who Annabelle is and where she is.

Brock, I wish I had been a father. I wish I had been a father to you and to Annabelle. I wasn't, and I am truly sorry. May your life be blessed. If Will and Matt made it through, please tell them it was an honor to ride with them. Please tell your mother I regret so much and that she truly was the love of my life. That part, at least, was true.

Please tell Ray I enjoyed breakfast and had looked forward to dinner and tell Sophie I would have liked to have been at her wedding—and as many anniversaries as I could. And last, please tell Huck that this morning was the most enjoyable meal of my entire life and that if a man can possibly fall in love with a grandson in an hour, then that is what happened to me.

Dusty

And so, I find myself, on the happiest day of my life, with tears streaming down my face. I look up to see that I'm not the only one.

"Sophie, I…"

She wipes away her tears. "Of course you have to go get her."

"I'll leave this week for Tucson, if that's OK."

She sits up a little straighter, takes my hands with both of hers and says, "*We'll* leave this week for Tucson."

And before I can say a word, to tell her how dangerous the trip is or to ask about the school or anything else, she gently shakes her head. "We'll talk about it tomorrow."

If I didn't know it before, I know it now—married life is going to be different, and it's me that's going to be doing some adjusting. As I start to think about that, Sophie, without another word, stands up and walks me into the house.

We walk past my old bedroom, toward hers, toward ours.

~ The End ~

57562737R00118

Made in the USA
Middletown, DE
31 July 2019